THE SHARP TIME

MARY O'CONNELL

THE SHARP TIME

DELACORTE PRESS

Grateful acknowledgment is made to HarperCollins Publishers for permission to reprint "The Monk's Insomnia" from *The Throne of the Third Heaven of the Nations Millennium General Assembly: Poems Collected and New* by Denis Johnson, copyright © 1969, 1976, 1982, 1987, 1995 by Denis Johnson. All rights reserved. Reprinted by permission of HarperCollins Publishers.

Visit us on the Web! or www.randomhouse.com/teens

Educators and librarians, for a variety of teaching tools, visit us at www.randomhouse.com/teachers

Library of Congress Cataloging-in-Publication Data
O'Connell, Mary.
The sharp time / Mary O'Connell. — 1st ed.
p. cm.
Summary: In the week following her mother's death in a freak accident, eighteen-year-old Sandanista Jones finds small measures of happiness even as she fantasizes about an act of revenge against an abusive teacher at her high school.
ISBN 978-0-385-74048-7 (hc : alk. paper) — ISBN 978-0-375-98948-3 (glb : alk. paper) — ISBN 978-0-375-89929-4 (ebook)
[1. Grief—Fiction. 2. Revenge—Fiction. 3. Teacher-student relationships—Fiction. 4. Interpersonal relations—Fiction. 5. Vintage clothing—Fiction. 6. High schools—Fiction. 7. Schools—Fiction.] I. Title.
PZ7.O2166Sh 2011
[Fic]—dc22
2010044170

The text of this book is set in 12.5-point Filosofia.

Printed in the United States of America
10 9 8 7 6 5 4 3 2 1
First Edition

For Steve Hill, forever

and

Dedicated to the memory and spirit

of Nick Givotovsky

MONDAY

THE FEAST OF THE EPIPHANIES

Anybody can tell that the pretentious ass who runs the Pale Circus fancies himself an artiste of sorts: a purveyor of poplin and mohair, an architect of nostalgia. A man of his station can't be bothered with the workaday minutiae of references and social security numbers, and so instead of a regular xeroxed job application, he gives me a Big Chief tablet and a handful of pastel-colored pencils.

"I want to know who you *are* . . . your essence . . . . your, your *thing* . . . ," he says, his voice cryptic, trailing off. Mr. Mystical! His eyes are pale, green as celery; his breath is fruited with Altoids. He has the pomposity of a great beauty, which, to be fair, he most certainly is. "Tell me why you want to work here." He strikes his hand to his heart when he says *here,* as if I'm a freelance cardiologist.

I give him a smile of supplication and hug the tablet to my chest.

He leans back in his chair and looks at me as if seeing me from some great distance, a squinting, owlish lover wondering: *Who, who, who are you?*

He is seated behind the blond oak desk that holds an old-fashioned cash register, a foot tall and scrolled in bronze. I already know it will make the actual coin-clash *ka-ching!* sound when the Sale key is struck. Candy is on either side of the cash register: a mahogany box filled with delicate chocolates and a cut-glass bowl of circus peanuts, coral-colored and chewy and filling the shop with the candied dreamscape fragrance of Easter lilies and marshmallows. The Pale Circus is entirely without the usual ground-pepper-and-hair-oil scent of vintage clothing shops. Breaking up the sugary aesthetic is a postcard-sized print of Edvard Munch's *The Scream* taped to the back of the cash register; above the howling figure's open mouth there is a Magic-Markered word bubble that proclaims CREDIT CARDS NOT ACCEPTED. CASH AND CHECKS ONLY, PLEASE. The walls are painted the soft coral of the circus peanuts, so that the Pale Circus glows with the otherworldly sweetness of man-in-the-moon honeycomb.

Mr. Pale Circus startles me by leaning forward in his chair. In an urgent tone more appropriate for alerting someone that her pants are on fire, he demands: "I want to know why! Tell me *precisely* why clothes are important to you!"

This of course seems like a test, which it probably is. Probably everyone who likes to shop at the Pale Circus dreams of working here. I wish I'd gone home first to change out of my school clothes. *School clothes.* It makes me sound like I'm wearing a smock top and corduroys, when in fact I am wearing a vintage red swing coat over some basic black. Still, had I known what the morning held, I would have dressed more carefully.

"Oh! Okay!" I take a deep breath that hurts my ribs. Not the entire skeletal cave, just that one spot. "Um, clothes are important to me for so many reasons. God, about a million reasons—"

He wags his finger, cutting me off. Tragic, as I was about to go all Marcel Proust on his ass, with varied tales of the poignancy of peacoats, of the chlorinated smell of swimsuits flung over the shower rail, which is pure August, pure aquamarine. I might have told him about my mother's winter white angora sweater, worn to fluff and gossamer, the remaining grid of yarn at the elbows so full of memories that if it could, the sweater would certainly open its mother-of-pearl button mouth and rasp: *Recherché, recherché.*

He puts his fingers to his lips and reaches out for my hand. He pulls my fingers back taut and with his thick forefinger writes on my palm. I try to smile casually—all righty then!—as if this is the most standard gesture between near strangers, but after a few seconds I fall into it and live in the creep-show ecstasy of this moment. He writes along each finger, a baroque cursive with deep curlicues; he wreathes my palm with—what?—ivy leaves, I think: soft, geometric, replicating. Oh, I am paying attention, yes I am. I am Helen Keller to his Annie Sullivan. The pad of his fingertip is full and beautiful and slowing the bang bang bang bang bang of my heart.

I close my eyes. Valentine pinks and purples and wild navy blues swirl behind my lids: constellations of paisleys and polka dots.

The tablet that I hold across my chest with my other hand is weightless, a mere paper shield over my heart. He moves his finger down my hand. He presses his thumb to the heart of my palm. Just sixty seconds ago I was terrified to walk into the Pale Circus, terrified of forming the question "Are you hiring at the moment?" The rehearsed, quasi-British *at the moment* sounding completely jackassy when said aloud to another human being. And yet I had gone and done it, hadn't I?

The shock of my morning at school gave me the courage that allowed me to pull open the door of the Pale Circus: *O brave new world.*

"Write down why you want to work here," he says. Then he drops my hand and says "Now, shoo, you" in a school-marmish voice that I guess is supposed to be funny or ironic or what have you, and I think *Hey, shoo you too, pal,* though of course my hand feels like the softest firecracker and my heart is all agog with sudden cuckoo bird love, but I shoo, people, yes I do.

I walk through the maze of circular racks of clothes, a fabric kaleidoscope that I have perused many times as a mere customer, not a potential employee. At the door I pause to give a little wave, but he doesn't wave back. He is holding up a salmon-pink coat and frowning at the frayed triangular collar until he catches his reflection in the mirror and gives himself a lovelorn gaze.

And then I'm in the cold again.

Because I had wanted to gather my courage before I walked in and applied for a job, I parked a half block down from the Pale Circus on the opposite side of the street, in front of a pawnshop called Second Chance? The jaunty question mark at the end of Second Chance? seems to be a thematic joke that emphasizes both the inherent corniness and questionable promise of second chances: *Second Chance? You think?* And of course there's the standard pawnshop vibe, the seedy sadness of the candy-apple-red drum set in the front window, a single drumstick sitting forlornly on a high hat—some sweet little rock and roller down on his/her luck. Next door to the pawnshop is Erika's Erotic Confections. In the display window a white chocolate bust, a milk chocolate bust and a dark chocolate bust are demurely covered in bikini tops. I have shopped at Erika's once, intending to buy a gag gift. However, when I walked in and found Erika—six feet, whacked-off hair bleached white, tattoos and a black tank top beneath her chef's apron—glowering at me, offering up a tart and perfunctory "May I *help* you?", I looked away from the marzipan handcuffs and organic edible underwear and bought one of her artisan chocolates displayed on a silver platter in the cooler. The only other row building that is not boarded up and plastered with handbills is the liquor store on the corner—a liquor store that pains me, pains me, pains me—and then, at the end of the street of deserted blocks, is St. Joseph's Monastery, a towering redbrick beauty that sits on a hill like the gateway to some uneasy Oz: *Uh, so, welcome to the Emerald City? I guess? We hope?*

I unlock my car and grab my cigarettes from the dashboard and see that a pamphlet has been tucked beneath my windshield wiper: a holly-green brochure with three stenciled kings proclaiming *Happy Feast of the Epiphany!* in bloated thought bubbles floating above their staffs and camels. I think about the events of this morning and let out a bitter little snort. *No fucking kidding, wise men; epiphanies galore.*

I open the brochure and learn that this feast day is a kind of post-Christmas blowout: *Now, after contemplating the staggering fact that God has become a human child, we turn to look at this mystery from the opposite angle and realize that this seemingly helpless child is, in fact, the omnipotent God, the king and ruler of the universe.*

I jam the brochure into my pocket, thinking, *Omnipotent? Bang-up job, pal.* I take a seat on a bench in front of Second Chance? and choose a melon-colored pencil. I stick the other pencils under my thigh, the sharpened ends poking at my ass like a little bundle of arrows. Why do I want to work at the Pale Circus?

I love the clothes at the Pale Circus! I have no interest in new clothes. New is ever so dull; new can suck it hard. New clothes symbolize the exploitation of third-

world children locked in the factory, the modern-day slavery of the Mariana Islands, the workaday misery of Walmart employees. So let's try something else, please: meet me in St. Louis with a cardinal-red Judy Garland–ish cape and fur-trimmed muff! Help me to express my inner smiley-face decal of happiness in a Marcia Brady poly-blend minidress and stacked sandals. Make me a channel of your peace, if you will, in a rainbow maxidress, a strip of fabric saved for a red-yellow-blue-green headband, and, people, show me the woven hemp espadrilles. Hire me, please!

Thanks a trillion,
Sandinista Jones

PS I am available anytime Monday through Friday, as well as any weekend hours.

I put the tablet and the pencil on the bench next to me and light a cigarette. A low-riding green Buick rolls down the street, the circular slop-slop-slop of tires cutting through slush, a snippet of buzzy AM radio filtering out: *Monday, Monday, can't trust that day.*

Understatement.

The air has that iced mineral smell that comes right before new snow falls. I look across the street at the Pale Circus. The awning is striped, a wash of coral and cream, the letters pastel and swollen. In the window, a headless mannequin wears a purple-red taffeta ball gown—I believe the color could be called mulberry, perhaps raspberry—cut to a low V in the front and bolstered by so many crinolines it looks like she might levitate: one hand is already raised and fanning out. *Good-bye! So long!* The carmine-red flats on her highly arched feet give me the rainbow-confetti feeling of a happy ending. But when I look at the liquor store on the corner, that sweetness vanishes.

The liquor store was once a health-food store, the Sunshine Co-op, where my mother bought the natural peanut butter that all children despise for its grotesque texture of ground bones. But she also bought plenty of nice things: dusty raspberries and green beans, dark chocolate pastilles, pear-peach smoothies. The earnest hippie dude who ran the store had painted a mural on the side of the building, so that all who turned left on Thirty-Eighth Street would be greeted by a somber Cesar Chavez holding out a fistful of purple grapes. Painted over his head were the words WE'RE SOWING THE SEEDS OF CHANGE, which I suppose is true of both a health-food store and a liquor store. But then the organic superstores opened up in the suburbs, and people stopped driving downtown for organic milk and hemp lip balm, and that was that for the Sunshine Co-op. Except nothing ever snaps shut so neatly, there is no spick-and-span denouement, there is forever the image of my mother weighing root vegetables, standing on tiptoe in her espadrilles, peering at the scale's needle, then turning and giving me a brightly exaggerated smile, as if to say, *Rutabagas and parsnips and daikon! Oh my!*

I think of my mother and I can't believe this morning, this year, this life. I close my eyes and a wild paisley pattern flits along the back of my eyelids: purple, valentine-pink and navy blue figures; oblong, sperm-shaped, kidney-shaped. When I take a sharp breath in, the sore spot on my rib vibrates up to the back of my throat.

I heave myself off the bench and make my way down Thirty-Eighth Street, practicing for my upcoming conversation with Mr. Pale Circus. I make carefree hand gestures and mouth witty asides to the arctic Kansas City air, trying to perfect my confident girl-Friday vibe. Perhaps my aggressive cheerfulness is alarming, because when I walk back into the shop with my insane grin and my head held high, swinging my hair like a prancing Connemara pony on crack, Mr. Pale Circus looks at me and blanches: his shoulders shoot up; his mouth forms a fat, appalled oval. But when I hand him his colored pencils and the Big Chief tablet, he smiles.

"You came back."

His voice is authentic and unflourished: nice.

He looks at what I've written and smiles. "Miss Sandinista Jones. I would have hired you for your name alone," he says tenderly, "even if you were a serial killer or a chronic shoplifter."

But then he gathers himself. "Welcome to the Greatest Show on Earth," he says, doffing an imaginary top hat.

He hands me a Pale Circus business card:

HENRY CHARBONNEAU
RINGMASTER AT LARGE

He tells me to come to the Pale Circus tomorrow morning at ten o'clock. He shakes my hand. When I walk out the door, the string of silver bells trembles along the safety glass.

And then I'm back in the world, squinting up at the monastery and touching the middle of my hand again, the soft, meaty bull's-eye of Christ's agony.

Across the street, a monk walks by in his brown robe, his hood up, so that in profile he looks like the grim reaper. I wonder if he is happy, if his life is all peaches and rainbows and pretty pretty God love; I wonder if he sleeps with frankincense, gold and myrrh dancing in his head. Or does he celebrate the Feast of the Epiphany by praying all night, only ceasing when the sky finally gives up the violets of dawn?

When he looks over at me he doesn't smile, but he does wave. He lifts his hand and his sleeve falls to his elbow, revealing his bony wrist, his pale forearm. And it seems that this is the very moment when the snow starts, fat, soft flakes that fall slowly and silver: fairy-tale stardust.

* * *

But then there is getting though the rest of day, the aimless, creeping hours: smoking and drinking a latte at Buzz Café, thinking *Right now I would be in American History* and then taking the longest way home, not along the gray sweep of the interstate, but through the bisected heart of the city, where I slowly drive past St. Scholastica's—a doll of a school, all pearl-colored brick and sweet girl-saint statuary—the school where my mother wore Doc Martens and ripped fishnet stockings with her black watch skirt, where she reapplied liquid eyeliner and smoked weed in the bathroom before religion class so that the saints would tiptoe out of the oil paintings and whisper epiphanies, their candied breath at her ear, their muslin robes brushing her bare knees, her white cotton socks. I say right out loud in the cold car: *"Help me Help me Help me."*

Of course, it's a made-up prayer, nonfancy and pathetic, because I am not a Catholic, because my mother was no longer Catholic by the time I came along, and chose not to have me baptized. My grandparents were devout, but they lived in Florida, and I saw them only twice a year when I was a child. My cultural Catholicism is specific and spotty, highlighted by delicious ghost stories whispered by my grandmother while we roasted marshmallows over a beach bonfire: "St. Lucy gouged out her eyeballs for Christ!" My mother and I attended the Zen Center and many Christian churches, her favorite being the Unitarian church with the optimistic banners hanging in the sanctuary: FEELINGS ARE NEITHER GOOD OR BAD—THEY JUST ARE! I'M REAL SPECIAL CUZ GOD DOESN'T MAKE JUNK. My mother was mildly troubled by the poor grammar and corn-dog aesthetic, but mostly she was happy that I had "the opportunity to see Jesus as a brother, not as Big Daddy."

As St. Scholastica's disappears in my rearview mirror, I'm thinking of my teenage mother—plaid-uniformed, Marlboro in hand, all her requisite madcap antics—and I'm not paying attention and there's the blare of horns and squealing brakes behind me but in the next second I'm still completely alive.

* * *

And then there's coming home but not walking into the house right away, just sitting on the freezing porch swing and smoking before walking around to the backyard—the kidney-shaped flower beds crunchy with ice-glazed leaves, the chain-link fence a geometry of snowy iron diamonds—before I go in the back door and move from the January cold to subtropical heat. I forgot to turn the heat down after I took my shower this morning. *Guess who's not paying attention?* Yet again.

And there is the big surprise of the cool gray button on the answering machine. I was expecting the wild siren flash of multiple missed messages: maybe not the police, but at least the principal, the counselor, my Honors English teacher, Ms. Lisa Kaplansky. A friend or two. But no.

And so I eat a fun-sized Almond Joy and pace around for an hour; I watch TV and wait for the official phone calls. On the Discovery Channel, a cheetah outruns a gazelle and plunges his openmouthed face into the gazelle's skinny neck. But after the chase, after all that pouncing and guttural roaring, the cheetah doesn't seem especially hungry for the body and the blood. The cheetah rests his claw on the gazelle's open chest and licks its shoulder, nonchalant: *I just did that because I could, people.* I switch to the mind-numbing show where celebrities dance, and paint my fingernails black raspberry. When my nails dry, I lie on my back on the couch and put my hand under my shirt, cradling the hurt part of my ribs. I consider the water stains on the ceiling; if I don't blink, if I squint until my eyes water, I see the angel Gabriel with his arched wings and kind outstretched hands, his head cocked to the left, as if imploring me to get off my sorry ass and do *something*. And so I haul myself off the couch, switch on the computer and Google the shit out of Mrs. Catherine Bennett.

There are ever so many—a Playboy Bunny, a marine biologist, a birdhouse builder—but I finally find my own private Catherine Bennett. She teaches at Woodrow Wilson High School. She is a consultant on a textbook called *Math Without Fear!* She donated fifty dollars to the Humane Society in honor of the late Mr. Fluffers Bennett. She lives at 1207 Ponderosa Lane. I put her address into MapQuest, and while I study the grid of intersections and arrows that leads from my house to hers, my mind wanders to the image of me at school, gathering my books off my desk and walking out the classroom door, my classmates seated, unsure whether to stay or to go, and then the asthmatic gloom of the hallway, of searching for my car keys in my pockets and my purse and backpack, waiting for the small relief of metallic shivering and deciding that I will change my stupid fucking destiny, that I will drive away from Woodrow Wilson High School and apply for a job at the Pale Circus.

I call my friend Caitlin Jantzen and leave a message on her cell phone: "Bennett lost it today. On me. Freak show extraordinaire. Did you hear? Jesus. Call me." But my hopes aren't that high. I haven't returned her calls in months, and Caitlin has a new boyfriend in a band, a strapping lad, handsome and prehistoric, with high cheekbones and a large, commanding skull that houses a brain the size of a shelled walnut. I try to decide who to call next, but then the story itself is so humiliating . . . so I zone out and put on cherry lip balm, coats and coats of it, a soothing and useful repetition, thinking that my waxed lips will never chap, thinking: *Hurrah! I am embalmed.*

I walk into the kitchen for variety and stare at the mosaic of crumbs on the floor. I briefly consider sweeping and mopping, thinking it will be brisk and medicinal. Instead, I light a cigarette. I flick the spent match into the sink and exhale into the silence. Because I'm *paying attention* to potential fire hazards. I turn on the tap and let water stream over the match, over the stray cereal bits plastered to the sink. I'm not hungry for any specific thing, but I open the refrigerator to look at my mother's bottle of carrot juice, gone crimson and scalded at the top, a froth of pressed blood that makes me think of the body and the blood, of heaven.

I sometimes wonder if my mother has all-new celestial powers, if she can slice the roof of our house with one breath and float though the kitchen. I hope this is not true. I hope that the atheists are correct, that everlasting life is a mere snow-globe hoax. I hope my mother could not see that I spent Christmas Eve alone, curled up with a bag of fun-sized candy bars, worried that burglars would break into the house and gasp at the sight of me on the couch, silver wrappers littering the living room floor. I would be brave and breezy, saying to the burglars, to the world: *Oh, great! I knew I should have gone to my aunt and uncle's house in Florida!* In truth that invitation did not come, or maybe it did, maybe my uncle's elliptical "Whatcha doin' for the holidays, kiddo?"

was the opening, but I could hear relief in his voice when I told him I was spending Christmas with a friend's family: "Sounds good, Sandinista! There's no young people around here. You'd be bored stiff!"

I hope my mother is not looking down at me from heaven like an angel doll-baby sealed up in a plastic bubble, the most despondent Polly Pocket. My first day of kindergarten, my mother cried and held on to me, frightened as she was by the specter of crayons and glue, by my teacher, Ms. Kelly, who was moderate and kind. My mother would die all over again to see me mooning over her spoiled carrot juice, and I know I am lucky to have been loved like that, but I am also the biggest loser in the world to have had it ripped away, and so I smoke and pace and wait for the phone to ring. The moon is full and my rib is sore.

TUESDAY
THE FURNACE OF A STAR

Opening the door of the Pale Circus is like falling into a morning dream of a surprise Technicolor paradise: you walk up any old flight of stairs, open a random closet door and find a dance hall in full swing, a secret garden, a surplus of Starlight Mints. I have tried to honor the aesthetic with my first-day-of-work attire: I wear a soft pink mohair sweater (purchased at the Pale Circus back in October, a world away), a plaid pencil skirt, cream tights, chocolate suede T-straps and a waist-length raspberry fake fur. My hair is glossed and curled into a Veronica Lake peekaboo. I wear false eyelashes I had applied with tweezers and eyelash adhesive, and my fingernails are glittering black raspberries. I look like a glammed-up, wolfish Rosie the Riveter off her shift and searching for love: *Hello, you big, bad world.*

Today there is another Monsieur Cool manning the cash register and the candy dishes. This one is younger, lots younger, around my age, but going retro with his angst: he has on a vintage Sex Pistols T-shirt, Levi's with a two-inch rolled cuff and black motorcycle boots. I've seen him many times when I was shopping here—when I was a mere consumer—and I have sensed that he is one of my tribe: ADD, lovelorn. He has dyed licorice-black hair, and a fat Elvis-y pout. He gives me a solemn, unblinking stare. And so I follow the golden rule. Don't smile at someone until they smile at you first. Don't ever wave like a jackass, How-*dee!* Be forever cool. Aloofness is your friend, your BFF.

I stare back at him; we lock into a battle of neutrality as I walk across the hardwood floor of the Pale Circus. It's all *Whatever, fool,* until I am distracted by a display of vintage accessories. I see a golden compact—I'm guessing from the 1940s—scrolled with hearts and crosses, the sweetest iconography, and I imagine the circle of desiccated powder in the compact, a perfumed ghost of melancholy. I imagine the GI brides, all the Sadies and Goldies powdering their noses before heading out to the dance floor to jitterbug in stacked heels, and my own shoes on the gleaming floor of the Pale Circus make the soft, golden click of the compact snapping shut, over and over and over.

So maybe my own life is not so drastic and dreadful . . .

maybe I am just like all those other girls who have come before me with their oily T-zones and random terrible days and bittersweet triumphs, the world billowing out behind them.

I glance again at the boy—I am but a foot from the cash desk—but then, on the circular rack to my left, I notice a white leather jacket with a fat silver buckle at the waistline and then—whooooosh—I'm riding down Carnaby Street on the back of a skinny boy's Vespa, my eyes teary and squinting from the cold wind, curtained with waterproof Cleopatra eyeliner. My mother appears and waves madly at the lovebirds on the Vespa; she's mod as you please in a *Quadrophenia*-style army jacket and black leggings. I'm not in the Pale Circus, I have left Kansas City and now live in the London of my dreams for ten sweet seconds and of course *I'm not paying attention;* I'm daydreaming the lost future my mother and I had planned. When I finished school in May, we were going to sell the house and spend a year traveling in Europe. College could wait, she said. Her own freshman year had consisted of arguing with her bitchy roommates and mooning over her biology TA. She believed my own dorm-room dramas could be put on hold for a year or two while we grooved on life in Europe. But of course, nothing could wait, and now the world sparkles on without my mother.

When I look back up at the real boy, we have five more seconds of Coolfest USA, but then it's as if we've both been tapped by the same lightning rod of goofiness. We suddenly smile at one another, not proper social smiles, but wide, stupid ones: gums prominently displayed, throats wreathed with impending laughter.

"Hello," I say. Closer, I see that he might be older than me. Not by much. A few years? He has charming crinkles around his brown eyes that hint at copious nicotine consumption and . . . could it be? . . . tanning beds.

"Hello," he says, imitating my soprano tone, my congeniality. And so I have my social cue to let the games begin.

"I think I am a new employee," I say, employing a musical accent of no discernable origin.

"Indeed," he says, "you are the new girl." On the desk in front of him are vintage valentines, hundreds of them, scalloped and sepia along the edges. Sweet Jesus, Valentine's Day! Next month's doomsday holiday. But compared to Christmas, Valentine's Day seems good-hearted, communal: there will be many, many blue people eating chocolates by themselves and watching bad TV.

He gently stacks the valentines and puts them in a shoe box. He very officiously claps his hands, then takes a circus peanut out of the bowl next to the cash register, holds it up to me, Communion-style, and smiles. "Greetings, new girl."

And so I am the new girl, pierced with—well, I'll be goddamned—happiness as I think of my fellow students, my "friends" at Woodrow Wilson High School, who are already in class and wearing their jeans and T-shirts, their bright sweatpants ensembles and their flat boots with soles like pork cutlets that are currently the rage among the blond and dullardly masses. Oh, if they could see me now, that old gang of mine! My nails are perfectly arched blood-black roses, and as I reach out to take the coral candy, what I think is this: the aesthetic of my life has improved about one hundred and five percent.

But then the boy yanks the candy back and whisper-shrieks: "Never, ever touch one of these. Seriously, you'll get hepatitis B. Or C. You'll get the goddamn *alphabet* of hepatitis." He returns it to the bowl with a shudder, then gives me a brilliant smile. "People think: Hotmotherfuckin' damn, free candy, circus peanuts, well, holy smokes. My parents loved circus peanuts when they were kids. Ooh, how very charmingly retro, how admirably thematic. Yum!" He shudders. "They stick their hand in the bowl: filthy fingers, scabby cuticles. Sure, they've just pumped gas or used the facilities; sometimes they grab for a circus peanut *whilst,*" he says, making his voice schoolmarmish for that one beat, "they are picking their nose."

"Yum," I say. "Delish."

He takes a chocolate from the mahogany box next to the circus peanuts. "These, however, are too good to resist. The woman across the street makes them." I want to say that I am well aware of Erika's Erotic Confections, that I know a thing or two about Thirty-Eighth Street, but then who likes a know-it-all? He holds the box out to me, and though I don't really want any communal candy after the germ lecture, I pop a chocolate in my mouth anyway: rum, vanilla, cinnamon, the center a surprise of crumbling meringue . . . it's like a piece of pie jammed into a chocolate. I offer up an orgasmic eye roll.

"Right? Mmm . . . Moroccan Meringue." We chew our chocolates, and the slight bob of his Adam's apple tells me that we are swallowing in unison.

"So. I've only seen you in here about a million times."

I have the joy of remembrance, of recognition; my heart a muscled little purple cow jumping over the moon, my throat coated with sugar.

"So what's your name, new girl?"

I hesitate before I rock the nickname: "I'm Sandi."

"As in Beach? As in Duncan?" He chortles. He must assume I'm devastated by his minor witticisms, because he follows up with a quick "Hey, I'm not winning any prizes in the name department either. My name is Bradley." He motions holding a baby, rocking it back and forth. "What shall I call my little prince: Ian? Jonathan? Holden? Uh . . . no, those all sound kind of tacky. I'm going for Bradley. I'll call him Brad! How sonorous, how very magical: Braaad."

I laugh, loud and horsey. "Brad!"

He rewards me with a smile; he holds his hand out to me. "Nice to meet you, Sandi."

"As in Nista!" I say. "Nice to meet you, too." His grip is perfect, neither too tight nor too loose.

"Sandi?" He opens his eyes wide. He says my name again, this time with a short *I*. "Sandi? Nista? Sandinista!"

Back in the day, my mother wore a safety pin in her nostril, Siouxsie Sioux eyeliner and leather pants. She jammed out to the hard-core bands and the political bands, and her favorite was the Clash. She named me after their seminal album *Sandinista!* She was deeply drawn to their lead singer, Joe Strummer, not in any random whorebag groupie sort of way, but in the way of loneliness, of poetry.

I shrug. "My mother loved the Clash."

"Is there an exclamation point at the end?"

"I don't sign my name with it, generally. But it's on my birth certificate and my driver's license."

And here he loses any vestige of ironic composure. He says, "God, that is awesome! You must be so grateful to your mom that you're not some random Katie or Megan."

Despite the laughter at roll call, the *tsk, tsks* from teachers, the jokes my mother and I endured about the possibility of her giving birth to a second child and naming it Contra—ha, ha—in this moment I *am* actually grateful for her originality.

"Say, Sandinista, do you smoke?"

I hedge, in case he's a nicotine Nazi.

"Occasionally," I say. "I smoke every now and then."

"Well, then, God made you perfect. And so before you take off your coat and get comfortable"—he puts on his leather jacket, makes an exaggerated hand flourish—"Follow me, m'lady!" and leads me out of the Pale Circus.

I am stoned on the minutiae of new friendship: a one-inch crucifix tattooed on his thumb, a slight stagger to his gait that suggests a knee injury, the back of his neck, which he shaves—though not this morning—peppered with ingrown hairs. He immediately starts in on the owner: "God, is Henry Charbonneau from hell or what? I bet he made you write an essay instead of filling out a job application, am I right? God, Henry Charbonneau! Sometimes he'll read poetry while he makes you sweep and Swiffer. It is inhuman. Jesus! Henry Charbonneau! What a jackass. You're not, like, his . . . niece, are you?"

And I laugh and know that I will now always refer to the

owner as Henry Charbonneau, as Bradley does; I will never call him Henry. And as I walk through the Pale Circus I have a sudden burst of optimism that feels like love, love, love. Except that on the pastel periphery of loveliness, Catherine Bennett's gray pallor floats past. But an aggressively turquoise swing coat catches my eyes—a whimsical tigereye button at the throat—and I return to feeling fine and Bradley steps back to open the door for me and then we're out into the brightness of morning, the street in its snow-sparkle glory.

The sidewalks in front of the boarded-up stores gleam like silver skating rinks, but rock salt has turned the sidewalk in front of the Pale Circus to chemical slush. I mince around in my suede T-straps, trying to find the driest spot. I reach in my coat pocket for my cigarettes—the crinkle and luminous swish of cellophane against satin—and take out a fresh pack of Marlboros.

Bradley pulls a Zippo lighter from his pocket, the crucifix tattooed on his thumb taking a little bow as he sparks a flame. He cuts the awkwardness with a spontaneous French accent, saying, "Madame," as the fire hits my cigarette. A robed monk is walking down the street, swooping toward us like a dark bird, and as I inhale I have a moment of glitter-doll happiness—*wheee!*—that is the old snow and the monk and a new friend and nicotine and my dark fingernails against the inch of flecked tan cigarette filter. But again, Catherine Bennett is with me: she is the ice-cold blood pumping though my capillaries; her sociopathic smirk nestles in the blue vein at my temple and the wild paisley pattern of her slip imprints on my eyelids.

I exhale a cold plume of smoke and watch it evanesce into the winter air—doing my part for global warming, thanks!—and inhale quickly again, as if my body is only a conduit for nicotine. My rib hurts and Mrs. Bennett's ugly words come back to me, unbidden, verbatim. My mind floats back to yesterday morning, to all the slamming phrases I should have said back to Mrs. Bennett, those clever comebacks that would have made the class laugh and perhaps cheer for me—everybody loves the ADD underdog. I cough, I cough and cough, and my lungs hurt. My lungs are jammed full of tiny metal hammers and miniature barbecue grills that hiss and sputter and I wonder why I didn't simply walk out of class when Mrs. Bennett started up with her crazy-bitch routine. I am not some child trapped at a subpar day care, I am an eighteen-year-old adult with my own god-damn getaway car. And so there is the shame of that, of sitting at my desk and just *taking it,* letting a lame insane teacher treat me that way. And as always there is my embarrassing loneliness, my general momlessness.

But there's this, too: Bradley pats me on the back, prim and sweet, and says, "Goodness, that little cough could be telling you something. Such as: 'Congratulations, little lady! You've got lung cancer!'"

And like that, I can feel that the jumbled zoom and sway of ugliness is gone; for the moment, the creep-show allure of being Li'l Miss Tragedy is gone, and I laugh and cough some more.

Together we watch the monk walk the other side of the street. Squinting against the diamond flare of sun and snow,

Bradley puts on his sunglasses for a better look. The monk is twirling the braided white cord that cinches his brown robe, whistling as he slip-slides along the ice. He looks as carefree as the young Hugh Hefner twirling the belt of his satin bathrobe as he grooves around the Playboy Mansion.

"These guys from St. Joseph's," Bradley says, nodding at the monk. "My theory is that they're either on crack or lobotomized." He affects a stoner accent: "Like, dude, maybe they're simply stoned on the Resurrection."

"Creepy," I say, watching the monk.

He shrugs. "They're okay, actually. They're Trappist monks. They make the famous jams, the jellies. They're not big talkers. They are a *contemplative* order. They mostly just wave. I always engage them in conversation, though. You'll see."

I am stabbed: my mom loved the raspberry Trappist jam. There was always a jar in our pantry. And yet Bradley's magical *You'll see* pulls me into the candy-colored vortex of the future, a shared future in which I have a comrade with whom to smoke and study the midwinter habits of monks on crack and I have that sugar-swirled transporting feeling of happiness.

When the monk walks in front of the liquor store, he picks up the folds of his robe and picks through the snow on tiptoe, looking for islands of dry ice. He is wearing black socks and cinnamon-brown sandals.

"The footwear is a definitive lifestyle choice," Bradley says.

"Barbaric-chic," I say.

Maybe the monk senses that we're talking about him, because he immediately looks over at us and waves.

And so here is another surprise: not only does Bradley prove that he's not too sardonic and sophisticated to give a hearty, happy wave to a sandaled monk, but he also yells out "Good morning!" When the broken muffler of a passing van drowns him out, Bradley yells it again: "Good morning! How's it going!"

The monk breaks his vow of contemplative reflection or whatever to shout out: "We should all be wearing ice skates this morning!"

It's clear that we should all be wearing anything but sandals, that ice skates really would be a better choice, and in the next minute Bradley will quietly say, "He'd probably enjoy trading in the robe for some peacock-blue sequined stretch pants," and I will say, "I do so *love* the Ice Capades," and the two of us will smoke and chuckle in the crystalline cold.

But for this moment, which is all we fucking have, Bradley smiles at the monk. "Absolutely!" he shouts out, his cold breath spangling the air. "Ice skates! Yes!"

*　*　*

Bradley is the sweetest teacher. He is every inch the anti–Catherine Bennett as he starts the workday by explaining the geometric aesthetic of the store: He actually uses the phrase "geometric aesthetic of the store" instead of the trendy and more concise *feng shui,* which makes me like him even more. The clothing racks are circular—no straight lines here—so that the store looks softer and more centered, which, okay, sounds not only highly mockable and pretentious but also not really possible. But now I see that the concentric vibe accounts for the dreamy feeling one has when walking into the Pale Circus. Plus, the sherbet-colored walls are not junked up with merchandise. They provide a sweet and unfettered backdrop for the gorgeous clothes, which, in my peripheral vision, appear to be in motion. The soft woolens twirl; they waltz. The bright cardigans and kicky skirts flamenco. And all the shades and fabrics give me a giddy high, my hollow head filling with the beauty of jewel necklines and zippy prints, with vintage polyester and pale green sateen.

And beneath all the dreamy minty magic lies the quotidian: a back closet full of toilet paper and paper towels, Windex, latex cleaning gloves, a mop and bucket, Murphy Oil Soap, economy-sized cans of Raid to blast the cockroaches, Terro for the ants and, horrifyingly, glue traps for the rats, horrible, maxi-pad-looking contraptions that must cling like deathly sleeping bags to the rats' backs. Of the rats, Bradley only shudders and says, "They are some candy-loving motherfuckers; if we close the store for even a day, we come back to a wicked rainbow of rat shit on the floor."

For whatever reason, Bradley trusts me.

He fills the cash register with money from the zippered First National Bank bag, and after he shows me how the cash register works and tells me to copy driver's license numbers on personal checks, he says, "You can do the register today, pal," the word *pal* sweetly reminiscent of black-and-white film strips, of a boy throwing a ball to his golden retriever. And so I do. The first item I ring up is a 1950s cherry-red dress with whimsical pink topstitching—an excellent combo of fitted and flared—and to the lucky college student buying this dress I am just any old girl, but she will always be my first: the sweep of pale gold hair against her shoulder as she pulls crumpled bills from the dark cavity of her black backpack, her violet sweater, her dark-rinse jeans, her nose ring, her bitten-down nails, her bleached white teeth, her acne scars, her courtly *Thank you so much* as I put change in her cold, cupped hand.

Bradley Windexes the windows with his back to us—the tidy squeak of paper towels against glass—and Mrs. Bennett is falling away, gone gone gone for all these fat and happy moments.

* * *

I drive past my school on my lunch hour, wishing I had pimped-out tinted windows so that no one could spot me. Because as I switch into the left lane that turns into the Woodrow Wilson High School campus I see it: the one empty space in the teachers' parking lot, the missing tooth in the crowded grin. Catherine Bennett's champagne-colored Toyota Corolla is missing.

I shiver. The school must have put her on leave while they get this situation figured out. Or have they fired her? In any case, her sorry ass is not here, and I wonder if she's on some heartsick vacation, listlessly tramping around a random Comfort Inn off the interstate, buying a Snickers bar and a Mountain Dew from the vending machine before heading back to her room to watch *Days of Our Lives* or a PBS knitting program, maybe some Larry King rerun if the guest isn't too trashy. Maybe she flips through the channels as she eats her candy bar on the bed, before she is seized with the bad feeling of *Oh, why did I ever.* Maybe she walks to the window and looks down on the parking lot, at her lonely Corolla with the sun-bleached bumper sticker that proclaims: WELL-BEHAVED WOMEN RARELY MAKE HISTORY!

I rest my face against my car window, the chill of safety glass, and I let myself go there. I let myself feel it: the expansive insanity of yesterday, of Mrs. Bennett standing at the front of the room, of Mrs. Bennett asking if I am *paying attention,* her voice quivering, lowered to a manly baritone, which further enhances her crazy-bitch effect.

"Sandinista, I asked you: Are you paying attention?"

Mrs. Bennett wears an itchy-looking tan wool skirt teamed with a brown boatneck shirt: a slice of beige bra strap shows at the shoulder, but she is clearly immune to the lure and promise of the underwire. She completes the earth-toned look with support hose in the suntan shade and Clarks shoes. Oh, her vibe is pure sack o' potatoes, pure math teacher.

I do not look at her face. I will not meet her eyes. I have an anorexic's discipline, the cold steel will of a cutter.

"Sandinista, do you even know how to pay attention?"

Her rage unspools so quickly, her dramatic dinner-theater soliloquy on paying attention delivered against a backdrop of green chalkboard. Her lips tremble.

Not mine. My face is a scrim of indifference: *Whatever, people.* But inside I'm all outraged Pollyanna adrenaline, all persecuted synapses firing.

Mrs. Bennett comes closer to me, closer still. The space between the two rows of desks is her comfort zone, the teacher's terrain. Her shoes squeak—*squeak, squeak, squeak, squeak, left-right, left-right*—as if dying mice trapped in the spongy soles of her Clarks are letting loose with their final battle cries: *Fuck the cheese, fuck the cat, fuck the mouse, fuck the perpetual scurry and worry, fuck nestling in a forgotten cherry-red mohair sweater at the bottom of the closet.*

And then she poses a query better left for freshman poetry journals: "Are you sleepwalking through your life?"

Catherine Bennett marches toward me with her fluttering colorless lips, her eyes wild behind her bifocals. An expression that holds both delight and a despairing rage that surely does not stem from a student who doesn't understand a problem, a girl who has not completed her homework.

Shouldn't she be a little mellower on the first Monday morning after Christmas vacation? Shouldn't she be offering up some postholiday goodwill after two weeks of freedom? Also, hello? The girl with the dead mother? I'm your target?

"Sandinista, you never listen. Do you need a"—and here she cupped her hands over her mouth, her fingers curling

into a megaphone when she screamed her last two words—
"hearing aid?

"All I ask is that you listen, Sandinista! Is that so difficult? Hmmm?

"All I ask is that you pay attention!

"I realize you're not even going to *need* algebra if you're
just going to get married and have babies."

I don't tell her: *Bitch, the plan was Europe with my mom,
not marriage.* Though the "non-math = excellent bridal potential" equation I find quaint in its antiquity—though it
brings an outraged gasp from many a young lady and then
it's all:

"Sandinista, are you listening to me? Are you even
here?"

Her voice rising and shot with a shrill, aluminum whistle.

Confession time: yes, I did not review any algebra over
winter break, as Mrs. Bennett so strongly advised. And
I'm certainly aware of the freakishly ironfisted manner in
which Mrs. Bennett conducts her algebra class. (The class is
composed of sophomores and juniors, a few irresponsible,
arts-loving seniors like me, a few meth heads, and Alecia
Hardaway.) It's my second semester of Catherine Bennett—
I squeaked by my autumn of Algebra I with a D—so I really
should have known better than to come to class unprepared.

So, yes, I should have skipped algebra class. I *would* have
skipped algebra had it not been for that old devil inertia. I
walked mindlessly from Honors English—the sublime world
of Lisa Kaplansky, of poetry and prose—to the roaring fire
pit of Algebra II compliments of Catherine Bennett.

"Sandinista, are you paying attention?"

And then the world splits into two clean halves: Mrs. Bennett kicks the leg of my desk. I feel a vibration rise through my body. I am tucked up to my desk, freakishly so—the fat man at the buffet—so that the edge of it gives my ribs a ringing jolt. And the class vibrates with me; everyone sucks in their breath and lets it out slowly, oxygenated waves and shimmers.

Even before her foot hits the floor again, Mrs. Bennett waves good-bye to her known life. Because surely a teacher cannot really live deep down in the heart of Crazyville, though they sure do like to visit that town, especially when they are the only full-fledged adult in the room.

As soon as Mrs. Bennett kicks my desk, Alecia Hardaway starts crying. Alecia, the slow girl.

That nice Sara Ellison who sits next to Alecia croons, "It's okay, Alecia, it's okay." Even as I listen to Alecia crying, a shred of genetically coded empathy tells me that it's not easy to be Catherine Bennett, either. It's not as if I don't see Mrs. Bennett trying a little too hard with her rhinestone American-flag lapel pins, her swipes of bronzy-pink lipstick; certainly being a dowdy fifty-something widowed schoolteacher in a suburban Kansas City high school is not the sweetest deal in the world. She missed two days of school last semester when her husband died, her only absence during my tenure in algebra class.

"Sandinista!"

Her breathing is ragged, vicious.

It would seem that our grief-ridden fall semesters—

my mother's death in September, her husband's death in October—would make us mourning comrades, heirs to the tender world of sadness. But in the weeks after my mother's death, Mrs. Bennett's disgust with me came into sharp focus. *Sandinista, I hope you know you just can't slide by in my class. Sandinista, that dress! Sandinista, I won't baby you with a B you haven't earned.* And look at her now.

"Sandinista!"

When *I* finally look at her, my body goes numb with what will prove to be a homespun religious revelation, some angel whispering, "Here it comes!" I drop into the black hole of nothingness as Catherine Bennett leans down and screams in my ear, *"Are you paying attention?"*

My shoulder pops up to protect my ear and remains there, a tableau of severe scoliosis, and then come some unpleasant little epiphanies:

I will never effortlessly lift a car to rescue some screaming soul trapped under a tire.

I will never fall out of a fifth-story window and land, unscathed and sheepish—I'm okay! People, I'm totally *fine!*—in a bed of pastel tulips.

Any guy that has sex with me before giving me ye olde "You're beautiful and smart but this is just not a good time for me" is safe; he will not spontaneously combust as he walks down the street with some shiny new girl. Because I will have my Jesus-y creep-show miracle, the old stone rolling back from the tomb, yes I will.

I sense someone standing in the door well before I look up and see that the cavalry has arrived in the form of Mr.

Hale, the Drivers' Ed teacher/football coach. He blinks like a hamster in the sun; his nervous smile is partly shrouded by a humongous porn-star mustache. Mrs. Bennett looks over at Mr. Hale. She has been looming over me, her mouth at my ear, her man-hands on my desk, and she stands up too quickly and provides me with a solace I will play over and over in my mind. What she does is jerk upright, and her skirt catches the edge of my desk.

Her hips are substantial. It is easy to imagine her in the morning working her skirt up to her waist, so you would think that getting the skirt off would involve some work, some breathless tugging, but in this miracle moment, God's grace grants me a dramatic *fuck you.*

Her hem catches on a metal hinge on the corner of my desk and her zipper rips and a button flies off, hitting the floor with a *ping!* as her skirt slips from her waist to mid-hip.

But I don't see any lumpy panty lines beneath her panty hose, because Mrs. Bennett is wearing a paisley slip of valentine pinks and purples and wild navy blues. As soon as I see it, I know my brain will remember the pattern forever: The oblong shapes, sperm shapes, the kidney shapes bordered by minuscule dots . . .

The class inhales in unison, a fat, sucking sound.

Mr. Hale walks over to Mrs. Bennett and stammers, "Can I be of any . . . ? Do you need some . . . ?" He gesticulates madly with his hands, his upper lip a secret beneath his mustache.

Mrs. Bennett pulls up her skirt and tells Mr. Hale—she whimpers, actually—that she's not feeling very well. "I had a fever last night, and my head still hurts. I thought it was my sinuses . . . but I'm afraid it's the full-fledged flu." She pinches her skirt closed with her hands and giggles like a deranged coquette. But then, as Mr. Hale leads Mrs. Bennett out of the classroom, she starts to cry: gasping, phlegm-choked. Everyone studiously looks away from me, except for Alecia Hardaway, the slow girl breaking the silence, trying to make it all better by shouting across the classroom: "Hi, Sandinista! You're a real cool person, Sandinista! You're a real cool person every day!"

And then it's me trying to ignore her delusional salutations, trying to casually leave the classroom as if for a dental appointment, and then running down the hall and out the front doors of Woodrow Wilson High School.

*　*　*

Before I head back to work, I cruise the student section, one hand on the steering wheel, one hand flattened to the sore spot on my rib, not wanting to be seen, wanting to be seen, not wanting to be seen, wanting to be seen: the Invisible Man snapping his rainbow suspenders and pinning an oversized KISS ME I'M IRISH pin on his collar. I'm hoping to see Marshall Hoopes or Kellie Brock in the parking lot. The digital clock on my dashboard says 12:25, so I know fourth period is breaking for lunch, and I wonder if Leah Carr and Caitlin Jantzen and Parker Jackson and Megan Loneker are congregating around my locker, wondering where I am, how I'm doing: *Where is she? Where is Sandinista?*

I imagine the teachers are tense and nervous, the administration confused and wimpy. I stare at the school and note how it resembles a penal colony: the grim redbrick nothingness, the extensive and regularly broken rules. I dig my cell phone from my purse and call my home number. When I enter the code and check for messages, there is in fact one new message and my heart does a scream-roller ascent—here it is, it's coming, the facts from the school, the deal struck by the school board and principal and would I like to come in and talk to the counselors and would I, perchance, be willing to sign a confidentiality agreement about the whole Catherine Bennett scenario? However, it is not anyone from school, it's a bored voice saying: "Stanley Steemer is having a sale on carpet cleaning this month, four rooms for the price of three." Godfuckingdamnit. "Imagine how terrific your home will look and smell with freshly cleaned—like new!—carpets."

I hit the End button on my phone. I comfort myself with this thought: I have to get back to work. Backtowork. Backtowork. Backtowork. The staccato comfort of it.

* * *

The afternoon passes too quickly, the Pale Circus precisely the heaven I had imagined. Well, a heaven framed by unringing phones and the ghost of Catherine Bennett, but then there is also the strikingly angelic Bradley leading me to the three-way mirror at the back of the store. Bradley holds up an A-line dress printed with interlocking aqua and olive circles and says, "You *have* to try this on," and, "How fun to work with a girl; it's like having my very own Barbie doll." When I look at our reflection in the mirror it is very nearly a bridal tableau, and Catherine Bennett recedes into a haze of arid beige nothingness, which is perhaps the natural habitat of high school algebra teachers.

At Bradley's insistence I go into one of the two dressing rooms at the back of the store to try on the dress. I take off my sweater and stand in my skirt and black bra, staring at the bruise on my rib cage: plum-colored, sepia at the edges and shaped like Italy. I press my finger to the tender city, Assisi, where St. Francis communed with the birds, and then I touch the radiant center of the bruise: Milan, where clothes are spun from gold, from the expansive minds of geniuses. I remember my mother tracing her finger over a magenta Italy on the globe and saying: "Assisi . . . Milan": the two Italian cities she most wanted to visit when we went on our European odyssey.

My mind stretches, litigious: Should I take a photograph of my Italian bruise? I should. But then I hear Bradley sing out my name—"Sandinista"—so I quickly pull on the dress, and bossa nova—ironic yet not, for I am pleased with the print, the waistline—out of the dressing room.

"It's perfect on you, as I knew it would be," Bradley says. He crosses his arms over his chest and smiles like a TV dad on prom night. Bradley! He'll work here for only three more weeks; he's on his winter break from college, home with his family, home to the Pale Circus. As soon as he told me, it occurred to me that I had not seen him in the shop since summer, since all was right with the world. . . .

I'm admiring myself in the three-way mirror, absently

raising my hand as if I'm hailing a taxi, when the string of silver bells shivers against the glass door and a homeless man enters. He's every inch the stereotype, with Grizzly Adams wild hair, multiple stained Windbreakers, aggressive BO and windburned face, and of course he wants to know if he can use the bathroom.

"Please?"

Bradley points to the words *No Bathroom* that are spelled out in shellacked mini-marshmallows on a small oak plaque hanging on the wall, Henry Charbonneau taking the candied Circus dream a bit too far. I never noticed this sign before; maybe my eyes were blind to this, wanting so much to see only the pastel magic.

When the man leaves, Bradley asks me, "Do you think people really believe that we hold it all day? That we take in no solids, no liquids, I mean, surely this whole 'no bathroom' thing is the antithesis of entertaining the angels unawares—"

And here I go on space patrol for a moment and consider *antithesis of entertaining the angels unawares*—and loving my new friend—whee! But even though I am *not paying attention not paying attention not paying attention* and my mind falls into Catherine Bennett country, I don't miss much because Bradley is still ruminating on the bathroom/homelessness dilemma when I resurface.

"Surely this turning people away from the bathroom business will come back to fuck me at the gates of heaven." He brushes his hair out of his eyes with his hand, the crucifix tattoo on his thumb flashing. "But when you have to scrub projectile diarrhea off the walls, it turns you into a real Judas."

I change back into my skirt and sweater, and when I come out of the dressing room I look at all the pretty clothes, a variance of color and style and era. I talk about many random things with my new friend and I feel what must be the alleged peace of Christ, a deeply groovy respite spent with a disciple who seems better than the real deal—kinder, less prissy, without the creepy beard and über-goth crown of thorns, and who, in his millennial human form, has a serious marijuana habit: Bradley takes a break every few hours and comes back haloed with that unmistakable smell, the briefest rock show. Oh, but the hours take flight and soon it's six o'clock and it's all *See you tomorrow* and *I loved working with you* and *Good night, good night, sweet prince* as he walks me to my car, then takes off down the cold sidewalk, a boy alone, digging in his coat pocket for his bag of weed.

* * *

What's there at home for me?

I sit in my car until Bradley is safely off in the distance, and then I stroll down Thirty-Eighth Street. I look up at the monastery, at the liquor store, the erotic bakery, the pawnshop. I think of the world never stopping, just rolling, rolling, rolling, and I have that bad sensation of my hands starting to feel strange, detached from my body, that all my moronic thoughts and blood and bones are about to ooze out of the loose shells of my wrists.

But I am paying attention to this sensation, yes, I am paying attention. I am a person and I am paying attention as I walk through the sidewalk slush. I look in the window of Second Chance? The store is illuminated by a single bare bulb in the front window. There's a jaunty YES, WE'RE OPEN! sign hung on the door. Because I have nothing better to do, because I have nothing at *all* to do, I open the door and go inside. The back of the store seems to float in semidarkness, and there is a heavy smell of standing water and bacon grease, as if the pawnshop is in the midst of a breakfast buffet/flood sale.

There is a smeared glass case of wedding rings to my left, mostly cornucopias of yellowish diamonds on thin gold bands. The price tags are strung on the rings by black thread, like tagged toes at a morgue. I think of my mother's tan, veiny feet—she favored vamp polish and sterling toe rings—and my chest tightens. And when the *Are you paying attention* song starts up in my brain, I have to admit to myself that I am not. I am lost as I gaze into the next case. Handguns. I think: *Now, there's something that has never been on my shopping list.*

I look around the shop and see that people pawn some fairly useless items: a five-foot ceramic camel, startled, caught in mid-bray, his jeweled halter studded with dusty amethyst and rhinestones, his teeth glazed a bright corn yellow. There is a child-sized motorized Jeep—Easter egg purple and covered in Barbie stickers—a snowmobile, a mink coat chain-linked to the ceiling, a scramble of power tools trailing frayed cords, an oversized painting of *The Last*

Supper with jolly disciples pigging out and a foxy brunette Jesus looking up from a platter of purple grapes, his smile tight, his forehead laced with anxiety. Mostly, though, people give up their rings and their guns.

The handguns in the glass case are displayed on grease-stained tea towels. And there is another glass-fronted cabinet, this one stately and cherrywood, tall as a grandfather clock and filled with shotguns and hunting rifles that look clanking and cumbersome.

But I'm no Davy Crockett, no Daniel Boone, I would not want a big gun, I would not want to kill an animal, I definitely prefer handguns. And in the next second my brain does a mocking double take: *You prefer* what?

I see what must be a girl's gun next to the black revolvers and pistols. It has a shiny, snub-nosed barrel and a sweet pink handle with ivory mosaic inlay every bit as luscious as peppermint marzipan swirled with cream. There is a closed-circuit black-and-white TV over my head and I look up at myself: a grainy, blurred girl coveting a gun. When I press my palms flat to the cool glass of the gun case, a disembodied voice asks, "Need any help, young lady?"

Which of course is an exercise in understatement, and then he appears from the darkness, a man in his sixties with a full sleeve of tattoos and a faded red T-shirt that says CHARLTON HESTON IS MY PRESIDENT.

"I'm just looking," I say.

He holds a Styrofoam coffee cup in one hand. A book is tucked under his arm.

"At the firearms?" He smiles, skeptical and amused and grandfatherly there amid all the junk.

And my mind floods with the image of Catherine Bennett standing at the blackboard with her chalk and her perpetual smirk; Catherine Bennett, the flashing red exclamation point to my nothingness. I travel back to algebra class like Huck Finn without the funeral, and I imagine that nothing has changed, that the school has decided not to fire her, that the class sits, placid and resigned, in their straight rows of desks. Catherine Bennett wears a teal blue Hillary pantsuit and the humble expression of one making amends until she looks at Alecia. In my mind's eye, Alecia Hardaway sits alone.

Mrs. Bennett's wolverine smile fixes on the dreamy face of Alecia Hardaway, and I know that no counselor or principal or teacher or paraprofessional is on their way to help. I have studied the ways of Woodrow Wilson High School and know that I am the chosen one; I must keep Alecia Hardaway safe.

Still, when the words come out of my mouth, calm and sane, I am surprised. I am in no way prepared and there it is anyway. I feel my victim's mind-set fading away, replaced by a new idea, the attendant breathlessness of a new idea.

The guns glimmer in the dim light; CHARLTON HESTON IS MY PRESIDENT.

"I'm in the market for a handgun. I live alone and I need some protection."

The word *protection* is suddenly so reminiscent of condoms or birth control pills that I feel myself blush, a hotness in my neck that rises to my hairline and fries my scalp.

He looks at me. "What are you, sixteen, seventeen? Why do you live alone?"

"I'm eighteen, actually." And then I whore out my grief; I sing it out, slicing up the syllables: "Well, my mother died."

He chews tobacco. He says, "No dad around?"

"I don't have a dad," I say.

He gives a sidelong glance as if I am a child of a random hooker in a latex miniskirt, a glance that makes me want to smash the glass and grab a gun.

"You'll need to go to school," he says, looking troubled. He must be some kind of mystic, someone who, in this dank shop with its smell of basement water, can divine the lives of his customers.

I look down at the case of handguns. A wandering crack in the glass is sealed off with a strip of yellow wax.

"I'm not going back to school." I shrug. "School is not my thing. I had a big, big problem with algebra." I let loose with a psychotic little chuckle.

He looks at me for a long moment, an O.K. Corral moment, and then he spits tobacco into the Styrofoam cup. "*Gun* school, dolly."

Dolly, I think. *Well, hello.*

"Gun school," he repeats. "You need to learn to fire a gun, or in an emergency you'll end up shooting your fool foot off." He gives a masterful suck to his front teeth: *tsk, tsk.* "Very common occurrence among rookies."

"Gun school? You mean, like, a shooting range?"

"Something like that, dolly." He gazes out the front window and then gives a little forward jab with his shoulder. "You like working yonder at the used-clothes store?"

The used-clothes store. Henry Charbonneau would fall down dead at the sweatpanted sound of it. He prefers the term *spun-sugar vintage couture.*

"Oh, I like it a lot," I say. "I love it so far."

"Today was your first day, right? Thought I saw you pop in first thing Monday morning. I knew you were looking for a job. You didn't have the lollygagging shopping look. Dolly, you looked *all* business."

Perhaps he registers some alarm on my face because he says, "Now, don't worry, dolly. I'm no stalker. We keep pretty good tabs on each other on Thirty-Eighth Street, that's all."

Through the grimy windows I see a monk strolling past. Not the sleek handsome one. This monk is doughy and bearded and troubled-looking, a frown pinched between his eyebrows. The monk squints into the store. I know it looks dark from the outside; I know that he probably can't make out our forms, but he waves anyway. This hopeful waving seems to be the social contract of the Trappist monks of Thirty-Eighth Street.

"I'm Arne, by the way."

"Nice to meet you. I'm Sandinista."

He squints his eyes, as if thinking, *Well, goddamn if that ain't a doozy of name,* right before he surprises me again.

"Listen to this, Sandinista. I think you'll like this quite a lot. It's from this poem called 'The Monk's Insomnia.'" He takes the book from under his arm and half-glasses from the pocket of his T-shirt, and reads:

> "*The monastery is quiet. Seconal*
> *drifts down upon it from the moon.*
> *I can see the lights*
> *of the city I came from,*
> *can remember how a boy sets out*
> *like something thrown from the furnace*
> *of a star.*"

He whistles under his breath; he takes off his glasses and puts them back in his shirt pocket. "God*damn*. Excuse my French. But, 'the furnace of a star'? I can't get over it." And now a pair of monks walk by with their heads down. Just when it seems they might be oblivious save for their God-thoughts, they look up and wave into the store.

Arne waves back, then shakes his head. "They were like you once, young, trying to find their place in this wild old world . . . now they've found their place, I suppose, but they still have the memory of being thrown from the furnace of the star. I'm not a Catholic myself, so I can't say for sure, but I'll tell you what, dolly, those boys up on the hill making the jelly appear to have some goddamn hidden depths."

It doesn't seem polite to point out that the monks didn't *write* that poem themselves, that the pretty and pointless phrases are a poet's trick. But then I realize he's fallen into the magic of words as I am apt to do, which makes me like him but also makes me wonder why my Honors English teacher, Lisa Kaplansky, hasn't called to check in on me. She called me over winter break to tell me how much she liked my paper on *The Awakening*. She took time away from her family, from wrapping presents and eating iced cookies, to read my essay and pick up the phone. Well, where are you now, Lisa Kaplansky? Why doesn't the *poet* call? And then of course I'm not paying attention I'm not paying attention. Catherine Bennett looms in my peripheral vision, standing in the half-light of the ceramic candle, her words hitting the Replay button in my brain: Do you not even *know* how to pay attention, Sandinista? Have I identified the problem?

Arne lays the book on the gun case. It is a library book, encased in dirty vinyl, a bar code on the spine. "I'm going to make you a deal." As if in some ominous after-school special: a "deal." He scratches the stubbly gray hair on his chin, a professorial gesture, and says, "I don't want you to be scared at night. That's not right. You should be out with your friends, chasing the boys." He raises his hand, a magnanimous gesture. "Or . . . whatever."

Well. Arne cares. It's weird, to be sure, but he just met me and he cares. I see this; I see he is not from the school of smiling bleached-teeth bullshit.

"I'm not too big on the gun laws. All right? Look here"— he takes a ring of keys from his belt loop and unlocks the glass case of handguns—"if you were a drug dealer you could get one just as easy, and so . . ." He takes the handgun with the pink and ivory on the handle out of the case and gives it to me. "I know I can trust you."

I hold the gun tentatively with both hands, as if it is a

hamster about to ribbon my fingers with sharp little teeth. It's heavier than it looks. "It's pretty."

"So it is." Arne smiles, pleased. He relocks the glass case. "It's yours."

This is a confusing transaction for so many reasons. I stare down at the gun for a moment while I try to process this last moment: Who hands out guns to teenagers? Am I part of some sting operation of underage criminals trying to procure firearms? Will Geraldo Rivera burst through the door with his microphone and handlebar mustache? It seems best to keep my eyes down and my big mouth shut and study the handle of the gun, the sweet swirled cream and pink.

When I look up, Arne has crossed his arms over his chest. He gives me the quickest glare. "Here's the thing: A person should feel safe. Okay? Sometimes your safety is here," He strikes his hand to his chest. "Sometimes you need a little something external to get you over the hump."

Inadvertently, I look over at the ceramic camel.

"Or the plural form, the *humps,* as the case may be," he says sternly, before breaking into a gray-toothed grin.

Arne digs around under the counter for a minute before he reappears holding a square box of bullets and a wrinkled plastic grocery bag.

"I can tell you're full of sorrows," he says as mere state-ment, not overstuffed with empathy or sympathy, no maudlin *Moonlight* Sonata for Charlton Heston's disciple. "But the sharp time passes."

He holds out his hand; I give him the gun. And then he

puts it in a plastic bag, along with the box of bullets. He takes his wallet from his back pocket and flips through a half-inch stack of business cards. "Here we go," he says. "The pistol range. Out past Harper Boulevard. You'll need some practice before you become one of Charlie's Angels."

"Thanks," I say. The card has the words *Protect Yourself* in shadow letters beneath the address and phone number.

"This is a gift. No payment necessary, dolly. Can you assure me you're not a felon?"

"Not that I know of." I give him a sort of bizarre, flirty smile before I realize that this is someone I don't have to attempt to charm. He appears to be giving me a gift, no strings attached, as he says, "Hold the bag from the bottom so it doesn't bust out all over the street. And don't do anything crazy with this. Okay?"

"Okay," I say.

"For you, I'm taking a chance. For you I'm bypassing the ninety-day waiting period. Because I like you. Because I want you to feel safe." He comes around the counter and hands me the bag. He puts his arm around me. Usually the old "arm out from an old guy" means he is interested in brushing your breast, oh so casually: *Pay dirt! It's a tit!* But this feels different, this feels . . . creepy, sure, but also, this feels like friendship. Normally I do not kick it with older gents who smell of hard liquor and peppermint and BO—Arne is a bit of a big, stinky mint julep—but I see that he is trying to improve the quality of my day, with his kind words, with his dreamy cream and pink pistol.

"Well, thanks," I say. I feel like I might cry, so I affect

some kind of cowgirl–spaghetti Western accent and say, "Mighty kind of you, sir."

"No problemo," he says.

When I turn to leave he says, "Remember, I don't want any problems. If there *is* a problem I'll say you stole the gun while my back was turned. I'll say girls are crafty like that. I'll say, 'Why, I know exactly where to find that little lady: at the Pale Circus.'"

* * *

One quickly learns that, even when depressed, it's difficult not to feel like a bit of a badass when in possession of a gun. And surprisingly the gun makes me hungry, the gun makes me ravenous! Which is good, I suppose, because the way things have been going with all the espresso and cigarettes even the skinniest of my skinniest jeans have turned into voluminous fat-man pants.

I own a gun. Perhaps I will join the NRA.

I drive through Taco Tico and order the enchilada special just like any other customer, as casual as any old high school gal with a gun and a fresh box of bullets in her glove box. I arrive home to no new messages on my answering machine—how can this be?—but I do have beef and cheese enchiladas and a pink handgun.

The house is boiling.

I forgot to turn the heat down *again* and when I see Catherine Bennett appear in my peripheral vision, looking at the thermostat with glee and preparing to start up with her standard nutbar "You're not paying attention, Sandinista" routine, something different happens. I don't exactly point my gun *at* Catherine Bennett; I hold it casually in her direction like a pointer or a pie graph—*Here's something that could happen; let's take a moment and look at the percentages*—and poof, she disappears.

The house is still hot, though, so I strip down to my bra and underpants and eat dinner at the kitchen table. I put the gun across from me, where my mother used to sit. The barrel points at the empty chair at the end of the table, the phantom winner in a game of spin the bottle.

The gun is nothing, really. It's merely a centerpiece, not unlike a cornucopia of plastic fruit. It's not a petite dinner companion whom I'm expecting to cough up metallic bons mots. But things have changed. It's not as if I expect that now the school will call me, it's not like my mother will ascend from her cold grave out past the interstate, it's not like some father/boyfriend/Christ figure will appear, rugged and flannel-shirted, offering up manly hugs and solutions. But now I have something beyond gloom and pure bewilderment.

I have a gun. And my mind swirls with unthinkable plans, dumb ones, to be sure. But I can see now that a person doesn't have to remain staggering and surprised, ready to absorb all the hurts of the day.

A person can have a gun, and a person can make plans with a gun. A person can, if willing to shed cowardice and complicity, execute their plans.

Catherine Bennett's smirk bleeds in my mind, but now

it doesn't feel so unnerving. It seems like she's more the pathetic character, an active participant in her own doomed foreshadowing. When I hold my gun in my hand, I feel an odd, calm strength, maybe for the first time in my life. Maybe this is how God felt in the prologue to the book of Genesis: haloed with anticipation, and capable.

* * *

After my enchilada feast I fall dead asleep on the couch under a patchwork quilt my mother made out of my old baby sleepers, my little-girl clothes. The raspberry wool of my favorite kindergarten sweater is pulled up around my face, and I think I will dream dreams of glue and safety scissors and recess and graham crackers and a book bag embroidered with a green worm popping out of an apple, but in fact my dreams are dreary and asthmatic: walking through endless narrow corridors, eating a hamburger only to discover, my mouth jammed full, that the meat is a charcoal briquette that crumbles to ash. When I wake at eight o'clock, my childhood bedtime, my gun-happy girl-self, has evanesced and I am back in the hole, I am back to staring at the dark answering machine, thinking: *Oh.*

Still, I try to hold on to the good feeling of the pink gun. I crank up the stereo, put on my mother's old orange velour bathrobe and then play Charlie's Angels in the full-length mirror on the back of my bedroom door. I apply lip gloss and Cleopatra eyeliner; I brush my hair and swing it back and forth so that it looks shiny and lionine. I purse my lips and raise my eyebrows, surprised as any girl detective: Nancy Drew discovering the hidden cave, the cache of gold bars in the treasure chest. Oh, my hand looks so, so beautiful holding the gun! Perhaps I will be a gun-holding hand model!

I decide that I will paint my nails the same sweet pink of the mosaic of the gun handle. And the pistol is a freedom, a new freedom, that goes hand in hand with that other new freedom of not being the thing that someone loves most in the universe, being free to come and go as I please. I ramble around the house with the stereo turned up loud, my back splayed next to the bathroom door before I turn around and point the gun at nothing; I hold the gun over my head as I catwalk down the hall; I swing it around low as I walk into the living room.

There is the soft strain of the telephone ringing, trying to break through the Clash's *Sandinista!* (Oh, yes, they're playing my song; oh yes, I'm singing along . . .), so I race to the stereo and turn down the volume. With my gun at my side, I stand by the phone trying to will myself to let the answering machine pick it up. Unbidden, my free hand reaches down. Here is the dreamscape moment; here is the reckoning. I offer up a breathless, heart-banging "Hello?"

"Is this Sandinista Jones?"

Fast doom: the caller mispronouncing my name, rhyming up the last two syllables with *vista*. I know it's no one from school.

"Yes," I sigh. "I am Sandinista Jones." I pronounce it the same way she did.

"Hi! My name's Amanda Peterson and I'm calling

tonight on behalf of Discover credit card. Sandinista, since you're one of our most valued customers I want to let you know that—"

I quietly hang up the phone. I tap the barrel of the gun along the black plastic answering machine. My mother bought it at JCPenney last spring after our old chrome machine broke. The line at the cash register was long; we were bitchy. Later we walked around the mall laughing at the stupid clothes in the windows, at all the lemmings shopping at Abercrombie and Delia's. And then, in a dullardly display of irony, we went to the Gap and bought jeans on sale.

Mom, I think, *Mom,* falling into the word, allowing myself to feel it everywhere, in my wrists and in my knees, a connective-tissue disease I've been trying to outrun with my very public mourning. My funeral clothes—a vintage black veiled-hat-and-dress combo, short black gloves—became a wardrobe staple, an ensemble I wore to school at least once a week last fall. Some days I would add a whimsical touch with red Chuck Taylors, but usually I played it straight with black slingbacks. At home I've anesthetized myself with TV, with the Internet, with the resulting fatigue of long nights spent with both. And after these past four months of not answering the phone I expect my friends to call? Even after I had, in a fit of holiday grief, sent my friends an email over the winter break explaining that I needed time alone to "process my grief," as the books say, and that I would call them when I was ready to join the living? I suppose I should thank Catherine Bennett for making it clear to me: I did not need to make such a spectacle of my grief. Because I really am alone. I'm not like any other senior at Woodrow Wilson High School.

And wouldn't it have amped up the action in algebra class had I pulled the gun from my backpack, creamy pink and cold as iron ore in my hand, and said: *Hey, thanks for asking if I am paying attention! As a matter of fact, I am paying attention.* And I am paying attention: I see, I've always seen, exactly how Catherine Bennett is, how she preys upon students she perceives as weak or different, and now I have gone and joined Alecia Hardaway's club.

Except for one difference: I have a gun.

And I hate to geek out and be Grammar Girl here, but a gun is the perfect noun for a singular pronoun: *I* have a gun. This house is where *I* live. *I* live alone, and *I* own a gun.

It used to be we: *we* live here, in this house, together.

But I try not to say *we* too much anymore, *we* being the word for my mother and me.

Because even though I am a cool girl with a gun, it is hard to believe that I am no longer part of a family. Thinking of my mother being really and truly gone, gone, baby, gone is still so *hard.* I close my eyes; I cradle my gun to my heart. The difficult part is learning to think differently: This is *my* house. This is *our* house. Our house is the one with the ancient Amnesty International sticker on the refrigerator, the house stuffed with crafts from different stages of my mother's artistic journey. My mother carried a green woven bag to the grocery store so as not to fill the landfill with plastic, and I see it now, pinned to the corkboard next to the refrigerator, looking strung out and worn at the handle. I am not my mother: I use the regular plastic grocery bags and then stuff them in the trash, not the recycling bin. I am not such a peace lover, either. Possibly no one has ever liked the feeling of a gun in her hand more than I do. I turn the music back up and I dance; I sway to the music, holding my gun to my heart. It's a portal into all the things they do not expect from a Nice Girl Like Me. Maybe everyone has a secret life, maybe even Alecia Hardaway dissects and reassembles her world each night, trying and trying to get it right.

I take a deep breath and I look over at the answering machine, hoping that somehow I have missed another call. But the machine is dark. I grab the remote and try to lose myself in a reality show, but I find myself merely fascinated by the spray-on tans of the women, the telltale spots they have missed, pale paisleys on their inner calves—*Yes, Mrs. Bennett, I am paying attention*—and I keep the sound turned low so I don't miss a phone call.

I had expected the head counselor, known for her halitosis and shockingly high high-rise jeans, to call *last* night, certainly by today. I hadn't expected the big gun, the principal, Jack Johnson, aka Michael Jackson—nicknamed, I'm sorry to say, not for his dancing prowess—to call. So fine, he's a prince, he's a pal, he's running the goddamn school, whatever, but surely the counselor, creepy Ms. Reiber, she of the optimistic posters on her office walls—WE'RE HERE TO HELP YOU, and the classic shot of the terrified kitten on the tree limb: HANG IN THERE, BABY!

So, where is she? Ms. Reiber? Why doesn't she call? Didn't Mr. Hale tell anyone what he walked in on? Did Mrs.

Bennett go home for the rest of the day? Did the other classes she teaches get to have study hall instead of geometry and calculus? Didn't anyone tell anybody? Is Ms. Reiber so lame that she just doesn't want to deal with it? O school counselor, O valiant dispenser of chocolate kisses, of sugarless gum, where art thou? I have seen her specific kindness before. After my mother died, Ms. Reiber called me into her office and counseled me to "pop in from time to time if you ever feel like 'rapping.'" This made me wonder if she also wanted to, perchance, smoke some "dope" or "stick it to the man."

I wanted to tell Ms. Reiber that if I felt like rapping, I would audition for the talent show and kick it old school with some Vanilla Ice. Because it's difficult to place one's trust in a counselor who does not realize that word choice is a critical component in interpersonal relations. Note to my fat-assed forty-year-old self wearing an earth-toned pantsuit spruced up with a candy-green silk scarf: *Do not use the slang of your youth. Do not ever try to be relevant.*

Additionally, Ms. Reiber asked about my father. And so, to top off my fresh grief, I was forced into an awkward exchange that was basically me explaining that no, I would not be going to live with my father, because, well, I did not have much of a relationship with my father, but things could always change in the future, etc. Ms. Reiber alternated between her made-for-Lifetime-TV caring look (extensive nodding, a soft-eyed gaze, a pressed smile) and her concerned look (slightly raised brows, wide eyes, mouth a grim line).

I felt proud of my concocted story about my father, pleased with the polite understatement. Because I was conceived at a Holiday Inn in St. Louis, after a Cure concert. My mother explained that there was drinking involved, a broken condom: ye olde story. I have a memory of sitting with her in Perkins in July, the day after my eighteenth birthday. After so many years of hedging, here at last was the story. She smoked and drank her endless cup of coffee, saying, "This was the eighties, Sandinista, when sex with a near stranger seemed feminist and daring, not self-harming and slutty. Actually, you know, in truth it's probably all those things."

Square dancers were sitting in the booth directly behind ours—old gals wearing frilly skirts and matching red vests. Their spiraling bouffants angled toward us as they silently ate their Egg Beaters and eavesdropped. I studied the pancake photograph on the laminated menu—the brilliant royal purple of the blueberry topping, the ivory clouds of whipped cream. My mom told me that my father would not be reappearing, as fathers so often do in wholesome family films, walking in the house with their faded jean jackets and stubbled jawlines, their tanned crow's-feet and manly apologies. I knew this was true, but it made me a little sad—I secretly wanted Dennis Quaid to tell me he would foot the bill for college and walk me down the aisle—but I mostly wanted my mother to stop *talking so freaking loud.* Those square dancers were very interested in her story. And then it happened. My mother put down her lipstick-stained cup and said: "Sandinista, you will be the hero of your own story."

Oh. My. God. The corniness factor. The clichéd optimism. It was beneath her.

Mortified, I kept staring at my menu and did not look up when I said: "*Okay,* Mom. Got it."

And so here I am—the hero of my own story!—slung out on the couch, heroic in my quest to relax into the numbness of reality TV. When I imagine that I hear the phone ring, I press the Mute button on the remote and hear only the sounds of the house: the heat kicking on, the hum of the refrigerator and the death-knell *clong clonk* of the ice maker. I look again at the dark button of the answering machine and feel a burst of rage, *Lisa Kaplansky Lisa Kaplansky Lisa Kaplansky Lisa Kaplansky.* She's the one I really want to call: Lisa Kaplansky. She believes in bold prose and will *not* be afraid to call me up and say: *What the hell is going on?*

I imagine her in the teachers' lounge with her colleagues, lingering over a day-old starburst veggie tray of yellowing broccoli and soft canned olives, pale, woody celery and carrots; the teachers staring at the last of the onion dip dried to crust at the bottom of the tub as if it were tea leaves in which they could decipher the meaning of their washed-up dreams.

Lisa Kaplansky! How I do wonder about Lisa Kaplansky: Lisa Kaplansky of the foxy husband and new baby; Lisa Kaplansky of the sardonic smile and excellent shoes who writes either *YES* or *!* on every page of my creative writing journal; Lisa Kaplansky, who, when my mother died, gave me a copy of *Wide Sargasso Sea* and also, though I first found it to be a rather conventional choice, the collected poems of Robert Frost. But of course I found medicinal comfort in his wintry poetry, which is grief itself—brittle and chilly and white gray, as far as the eye can see.

Lisa Kaplansky, Lisa Kaplansky, Lisa Kaplansky. Lisa Kaplansky, who, one week after my mother died, tried to point me toward the future: "You've missed a lot of deadlines for college applications, but I'll help you with the school options that still exist. Your writing is excellent, so in your application essays you should—how do I say this without sounding cynical?—emphasize your situation. I bet you'll get a full scholarship, even though you haven't fulfilled your math requirement yet. College admissions people talk the talk about students being well rounded, but they know it's bullshit; hardly anyone uses algebra as an adult."

My Lisa Kaplansky. I have Googled her excessively. She contributes to a blog about MFA programs in creative writing. Her profile picture on her Facebook page is of her random-looking baby. She has had several pieces published in online magazines. I thought her work would be a mirror of Lisa Kaplansky: witty and big-hearted, with flashes of compressed genius, but in truth her short stories and poems were just okay. And now it's day two of *no call from Lisa Kaplansky* and this is quite a hurtful surprise, and I wish I could spread awareness of this problem with a postage stamp featuring a bold question mark next to an unringing telephone.

But why won't she just call? Why won't the phone ring and why won't I pick it up to hear Lisa Kaplansky say,

"Sandinista? *What* happened with Mrs. Bennett? I mean, everyone knows that she's glimmering with craziness and that she's not good with the special-needs students—I'm not talking about *you*—and no one does a good goddamn thing about it; it's as if everyone is in collective surrender, but that nutjob Bennett has been acting like that for years and everyone knows and everyone just says, 'She's tough but fair,' or 'Her bark is worse than her bite,' which is bullshit."

I pick up the phone; I put it back down. Possibly in the half second the phone was off the hook the principal called, Ms. Reiber called, Lisa Kaplansky called—synchronicity, people!—and everyone was outraged, so soft and caring. Soon a Candygram will arrive, and then unsigned bouquets of yellow roses will appear in the kitchen, a secret garden of sympathy, because *everyone knows.* I take the phone book off the bookshelf—it is the most-read book in the average person's home—and I look up her number.

As soon as I see Catherine Bennett's number, I know it will imprint itself on my brain. I will have to be careful not to absently dial it when ordering a pizza or checking my account balance, because the number will glimmer neon green, always. I put the phone gently down on the receiver and go to my mother's room. I leave the hall light on; I don't flip the switch in her bedroom. I open the drawer of her nightstand and feel around for her cell phone. It's shockingly cold, and when I lie down on my mother's bed and hold it to my ear it's like a cake of ice to stop the swelling of a brutal punch. I have done the creepy wax-museum thing with my mother's room. No clothes donated to charity, no dusting. I'm not crazy; I'm not praying my mother will rise from the dead and be delighted to find that her room has not been ransacked. I'm merely sentimental and lazy. In the half-light from the hall, her dresser is a shaded jumble of jewelry and scarves and a photograph of me at five: a neighbor's kitten in my lap, a corduroy jumper and Mary Janes. My grin is scrappy, confident: *Greetings, world.* I've got no idea what's coming my way. On the nightstand, the last book she ever read is facedown, splayed open; my mother was a spine-cracker. The book is on Spanish coastal towns. I close my eyes and envision my mother and me at a noon-bright beach, a checkerboard of beach towels on the Andalusian sand, the foam and cold shock of turquoise waves.

"So much for that," I say out loud, to nobody.

I dial Catherine Bennett's number.

I hope she has caller ID; I hope the name *Heather Jones* flashes from the phone on the nightstand next to her bed. I hope Catherine Bennett tries to place my mother's name—*Heather Jones, Heather Jones, Heather Jones*—now, doesn't that sound familiar, who in their right mind would call at this hour, pray tell? Her sleep-scrunched face, her glasses on the nightstand, next to a glass of water. She's prepared if she wakes up thirsty. She always pays attention. I wonder if she looks longingly at the empty space on the bed next to her, but, no, I imagine she and her husband slept in twin beds.

The pauses between the rings go on for so long that I think I've been disconnected and then, the surprise of a hello.

Well, of course the bitch surprises me, lulled as I was by the ringing of her phone, of course I'm not paying attention.

"Hello?" No fear of a late-night call, just annoyance. The world giving her yet another headache. Who is this Heather Jones?

The phone feels freezing against my ear. *What is the word you say when you answer the phone? Alecia?*

"Hello?" An intonation on the second syllable, the long, aggrieved *O* tinged with sarcasm.

I will her to say it one more time before she hangs up.

I hope she looks at the name blinking on her caller ID display: Who is this miscreant, this late-night prank caller, this Ms. Heather Jones? I hope she Googles my mother's name and reads her online obituary: *Survivors include a daughter, Sandinista Jones. . . .*

"Hello?" And then the click.

*   *   *

Then, at three a.m, the phone. It seems I am hearing it inside my body, a ringing in my ribs that jolts me from sleep and offers a respite, a few seconds of insane hope. Because who would be calling me at that time? Only a crazy neighbor, Mrs. Cavanaugh. She is calling to inquire whether I have seen her guinea pig, Duchess, out and about. In her rum-addled and rambling way, Mrs. Cavanaugh explains that Duchess escaped, perhaps through the clothes dryer duct, maybe via the fireplace. I long to say: *Nancy Jean Cavanaugh, you are hope's bitch, for a five-inch domesticated animal will not devise a laundry room getaway, nor will it shoot up through the fireplace like a furry mini-Santa on steroids.* Instead, I say, "No, Mrs. Cavanaugh, I'm sorry, I haven't seen Duchess."

After a few drunken mumblings about how just because I haven't seen Duchess, it doesn't mean she isn't there, and to check in the garage, Mrs. Cavanaugh starts to cry.

The bad comedy of my life. I hang up, pull my mother's blankets over my head and sleep.

WEDNESDAY
FROG AND TOAD ARE FRIENDS

The first thing I learn on my second day of work is this: Bradley steals. The Pale Circus doesn't accept credit or debit cards—it's cash or check with ID on the barrelhead, baby. This is both an antiquated way to do business and an excellent one if you happen to be a quick-change artist. Perhaps it's the only way to do it if you are, like Bradley, a sort of druggie Robin Hood of the vintage clothing game. I am working at the cash register when *three blondish sorority girls enter the store,* and, yes, I fully understand that this is the beginning of a stupid sports bar joke and one hates to offer up these simpleton summations, the laziness of cliché and physical detail. Nonetheless, three blond sorority girls really do straggle in, all highlights and laughter, carrying designer purses as chunky and unwieldy as laundry baskets strung up on leather braiding.

Bradley looks up from the sweaters he's rearranging by color, the rack a genius wheel of black to purple to garnet and cardinal reds fading to pink and then white and ivory before the blues, the greens, the grainy rainbow of cream, maple and brown. He grimaces at the girls, and then rallies with the weakest smile. "Good morning."

A bright day, the sun from the front windows dazzles us all. I am paying attention, yes I am, and I have a slight song in my heart as Bradley and I exchange a snobby smile of derision: *Ah, yes,* those *kind of girls.* The three little pigs squeal at the dress the headless mannequin is wearing: a short, A-line shift constructed of a clear vinyl shower curtain and shellacked vintage mini-boxes of breakfast cereal (Froot Loops, Frankenberry, Count Chocula, Apple Jacks). The mannequin is also wearing Ziggy Stardust boots: cherry-red platform boots with silver lightning bolts racing up the sides.

The girls say: "We so want this! Omigod, is that not a total crack-up? Can we get this? Is it for sale? Tell me it's not just for display."

Bradley allows a second to pass before he dignifies their questions with a reply. "It's for sale. Let me get it down for you."

"No! No worries. We can get it!"

They grab the mannequin and roughly turn the headless,

molded girl to her side. They yank off her special dress. Anyone can see their inherent brutality. For sure these are the girls from the shower scene in *Carrie*; these three make the mean girls from *Mean Girls* seem like martyred saints.

Bradley looks at me and shrugs. He pins a Siamese cat brooch with glittering pink eyes to the collar of a navy blue cashmere coat, transforming a Talbots dorkfest to the ironic, the Hepburnesque. The blond girls leave the mannequin crashed over on her side as they hold the dress up to each other and laugh, and laugh, and laugh, their very own Cloroxed comedy show as they go tripping up to the counter. Bradley walks over to the cash register, but I hold my hands up and smile—*I got this one!*—because I am now the master of the register.

Bradley smiles and whispers, "Hey, let me ring this up, Sandinista," and there is the inessential mystery of his aggressively Altoided breath, and then it happens.

He smiles at the girls. "All set?"

There is a gaggle of yep, yes and oh my Go-*od*, we found the perfect thing for our sorority's hounds and hookers party.

Hounds and hookers? How can this be? How can they not see that this dress is fit for neither hound nor hooker, that it is a sugar-cereal Kansas City original, a throwback to the Factory days with a nuanced nod to recycling?

The least pretty of the girls holds out her American Express Gold card. (I smile at her and have a candy-colored elementary school flashback of trying to get in with the popular girls by offering them Jolly Ranchers on the school bus: "The sour apple is awesome, but the cinnamon ones are like a real fire on your tongue!")

Bradley taps the sign on the front of the counter, the Edvard Munch postcard that announces CASH AND PERSONAL CHECKS ONLY.

And the girls say: "What?" And "Can you believe they don't take credit cards?" And "Not taking credit cards blows." and "How much do you have, how much do you have?" And they produce three twenties, which they hand to Bradley with much sorrow. The dress is exactly forty-three dollars, as per Henry Charbonneau's inscrutable plan of never using a zero or a five in his pricing. Bradley smiles and hands the least pretty girl the change, not counting the bills or coins back, but placing the little pile of money in her cupped manicured hand. And then the girls breeze out the door, apparently unaware that three girls cannot wear one dress. Bradley makes a notation on the Big Chief Tablet where we record the day's sales. Then he opens the cash register, takes out ten dollars and tucks it into his front jeans pocket—no furtive glances, just business as usual.

Then there is the panic and flurry of me trying to act like *I didn't see* as Henry Charbonneau walks into the Pale Circus with a man as tall and good-looking as himself, such a foxy doppelgänger that you immediately assume that love or even fondness is an impossibility, that what you are seeing in tight focus is pure, distilled narcissism. But who am I to say? I am not ruling out the mystical. The only thing I can be sure of is what I see: Bradley slipping away from the cash register, Bradley among the sweaters, Bradley raising his face and giving Henry Charbonneau and his friend a quick nod, a "hey" of calculated casualness.

And of course I am well acquainted with that *hey*; it is the last word you say before you cast your eyes down and pretend that nothing is happening, that your brain is not a crush of *OhIamsofucked*. I watch Bradley watching Henry Charbonneau from his peripheral vision: Henry Charbonneau is all cheekbones and smiles. His arms are full of vintage dresses, a rainbow clutched to his chest. He looks surprised to see me, even though he wrote out the week's schedule. Henry Charbonneau heaps the dresses on the counter—a good day at the estate sales—and says to me, "Mornin', sweet lady."

His friend smiles at me in a comradely way, as if to say, *He's kind of an ass, but how can I help myself?*, and I try to conjure a knowing grin to convey that, yes, the handsome jackass in his native habitat, though perilous, is often irresistible.

"This is Paul." Henry touches the crook of Paul's arm, a tender, paternal gesture.

Paul keeps his sheepish smile going strong as Henry Charbonneau massages his arm.

I have always thought the phrase "his face clouded" a hilarious expression—*Baby, glue some cotton balls to your forehead and give me a great big cumulous smile.* But when I look over at Bradley, who is studiously buttoning up a Kermit-green cardigan, his face really does cloud, a gray shadow rising from his neck to his forehead.

Henry Charbonneau raises his hand to me, and says,

"Paul, this is . . ." And this is not his fault, but in this pregnant pause, Catherine Bennett looms in, her coffee breath flooding my face as she asks, "Sandinista, do you even know how to pay attention?" In my mind's bloodshot eye, I turn to her and say—politely, and with a modest smile: *Mrs. Bennett, please do not forget that I have a . . . what's the name of that metal apparatus that shoots bullets? Mrs. Bennett? Yoo-hoo?*

Poor Henry Charbonneau searches for my name in a brain so very filled with Henry. See also: foxiness of; see also: aesthetic genius of, etc. I feel Catherine Bennett's voice vibrating in my chest, in the bruised spot on my ribs.

I am afraid if I speak I will start to cry.

This is only my second day at the Pale Circus, so Henry Charbonneau's forgetting my name is totally understandable. Well, then again, he did hire me, which, according to Bradley, is pretty rare. Bradley says I was lucky in my timing because I walked into the Pale Circus just as Henry Charbonneau had enjoyed some kind of winter wonderland weekend with his new lover. I got the job because he had fallen in love, love, love, love and wanted to spend less time at the store. Although really it was Catherine Bennett's timing—her Monday madness—that changed the course of the week. Henry Charbonneau has Catherine Bennett to thank for his sudden freedom to wander the estate sales and stop at cafés for baklava and lattes with his new love.

"This is the new girl," Henry Charbonneau finally says. "Is she not a peach?" he asks, pointing to my melony cashmere sweater. "Is she not a little doll in the house of life?"

Already I know that Bradley and I will be mocking this

last phrase, and this releases me from Catherine Bennett's death grip. I smile and hold out my hand to Paul. "I'm Sandinista. Nice to meet you."

"My pleasure, my pleasure," he says. "Sandinista: Your parents must be Clash fans. I love that album! You're lucky that they gave you such a beautiful, unusual name. It's unforgettable, actually."

But Henry Charbonneau misses the dig. He isn't paying attention because a woman has entered the store wearing stiletto boots. He winces at every sharp *clackaclack* of the boots, worrying about pockmarks on the gleaming hardwood floor of the Pale Circus, while he makes a big show of looking at the Big Chief tablet, checking the sales. And in what I imagine is an effort to look whimsical and carefree to his new lover, Henry Charbonneau puts himself at extreme risk by popping a circus peanut in his mouth. All the while there is Bradley arranging the sweaters, his hands moving through the racks, fingers chapped from smoking weed in the cold, the crucified Lord on his left thumb, his face a raw radiance of pain.

I know this was my face the day that the words *mother* and *car accident* became key ones in my vocabulary, the day that I was not paying attention, paying attention, paying attention, the exact look I had on that drizzly September day when the state social worker told me that my new and motherless life would be . . . just like living in a dorm! Well, sort of like living in a dorm, an empty dorm. My new life with the house to myself would have to suffice, because, well, there were no guardians in place for me, and it was lucky—well, not *lucky,* but maybe fortunate—that I was eighteen and so while still eligible for some services as a juvenile I would not have to go to a foster home, the words *foster home* springing out of the social worker's mouth with the same cadence of horror one uses when saying *rape* or *leukemia.* My mom had bought our house outright with an inheritance from my grandfather, so there was no mortgage and I would receive enough social security to pay for utility bills and car insurance and groceries, and the social worker assured me that my school would work with me, that the school would be sensitive about my situation. And Uncle Richard, my mom's older brother, and his new wife, Pam, came up from Florida to help me with banking issues, with setting up bill payment over the Internet, the sadness of transfers—deeds, titles—accompanied by a strange smile of expectant happiness on Uncle Richard's face, as if I were not properly expressing my elated gratitude, as if I were neglecting to pump my fist in the air and shout, "The Taurus is mine, motherfuckers!"

So I'm feeling short of breath just thinking about it all, and the bruise on my ribs hurts, a little sun radiating a burst of pain, and I'm not really *paying attention* to anything. But what I see out the window is this: a monk is staring at the Ziggy Stardust boots in the display. One of his hands is teacupped against the window glass, and he's smiling— beatific and amazed—and indeed it would be the greatest day in the world if the monk came in the shop and bought the Ziggy Stardust boots. He could go down the street, his sandals dangling in his hand, the hem of his robe rising up and showing off the silver lightning bolts that race up the sides, the cherry-red platform soles.

Bradley is watching the monk, and I look over and see that Henry Charbonneau and Paul are looking at him too, and we all dearly want him to buy these boots, we all want something offbeat and beautiful to come crashing through the day, and I start to love everyone in the world—well, not *everyone*—and that's when a granola woman—poncho, scuffed suede Birkenstocks—walks into the Pale Circus. She browses through the jackets before she pulls out a buckskin-fringe number and gives a happy little nod: *Oh, yeah, baby, this is it.*

Bradley saunters over to the counter with the granola woman and, with a burst of understated drama, reveals his genius. Bradley rings her up in full view of Henry Charbonneau and when he hands the woman her change, he gives her an extra ten-dollar bill. The woman takes her coat—in deference to Mother Earth, she passes on the plastic bag we offer—and counts her change. Her long, oatmeal-colored hair blankets her face until she peers up like a blond mole, and says, "Uh, I think you gave me too much change."

Bradley winces as he appear to check his math, looking into the cash register drawer, and then rolling his eyes. He takes the ten-dollar bill the woman is holding out to him. "Math is not really my forte," he says with a humble nod.

And I see the inherent genius in this preemptive cash game—if there is ever a question of wrongdoing, it will simply be because Bradley is not good at math. Henry Charbonneau has witnessed him actively being not good at math, and it all makes sense to me, because clearly Bradley likes the weed and I'm not sure if the vintage-clothes game would keep him high.

Henry Charbonneau sighs in faux exaggeration. "This is why I'll never retire in Paris. This is why I'll be slogging off to the estate sales at eighty-five in soggy Depends and dentures, Bradley."

Granola Woman gives a twitchy, repentant smile, looking truly distressed that she may have caused someone any trouble—or perhaps it's just the adult diaper reference—and I long to say, *You, O Lady of Natural Fibers, are but a cog in the wheel of financial deceit.*

But then Henry Charbonneau puts his hand on Bradley's shoulder and gives him an apologetic smile for the faux scolding. Bradley blushes and it's all too much for me, I turn away and start digging through the stack of dresses on the counter. Henry Charbonneau does have lovely taste: a lime wool shift, a hot-pink polished cotton cocktail dress, a cranberry sateen dress with glass beads on the bodice and a tiny waist, an heirloom from the days before trans fats and fast food. I suck in my stomach even though I am at my all-time skinniest—105 pounds. Still, I shudder in solidarity when I see guys in Jeeps with their NO FAT CHICKS bumper stickers, because hello, those kind of guys would not like a skinny chick like me, and my thoughts zoom away because *I am not paying attention, I do not even know how to pay attention* and Catherine Bennett swoops past and graces me with a saccharine smile, her teeth plastered with cockroaches.

When I look up, Bradley is frowning at an acrylon sweater that is zebra-striped and has dolman sleeves. The sweater is not even attractive in an ironic way, but then, Henry Charbonneau does have a weakness for ugly-chic.

So I'm ruminating on an eighties acrylon sweater when I see Bradley reach up and touch his shoulder, the spot where Henry Charbonneau laid his hand. Bradley closes his eyes and rubs his shoulder, a delicate motion that makes me think of the circular radiation of tree rings, and the heat kicks on and the Pale Circus fills with the smell of wool and warm candy, the sweetest lamb.

"Children," Henry Charbonneau says, waving his hand at Bradley, at me. "Go get yourself some lunch." He opens his wallet and hands me a twenty. A bit of benevolence meant to impress his new lovah.

"Thanks," I say.

Bradley hangs his last sweater regally. He doesn't gun it to the front door like I do. He walks, slow as a moon man, offering up a backward wave when Henry Charbonneau chirps, "Bye, kiddos." Paul calls out, "It was really nice to meet you both."

* * *

And then Bradley and I are out the door to a cold cloudy day of old snow, the wind taking our breath as we walk down the sidewalk, the monastery at the end of the street looking like a magical hushed heaven where your earthly problems would melt away—ta-da! Except there is a troubling bronze crucifix hanging over the entrance, the face of Jesus in his lukewarm and perplexed faith, two lines of a metal frown pinched between his eyebrows, his mouth a neutral line.

"Do you want me to drive?"

"That'd be great," Bradley says. "Since I don't have a car."

We discuss our options—barbeque, that smoothie place that also does wraps—but my mind races away from the tangy delight of ribs, of spirulina berry chillers. I take my cell phone from my purse, offering up a quick "Sorry! This is rude, I know," and check my home machine. I have *no new messages.*

"Hey," I say. I try to make it sound casual, a jaunty idea that has just now popped into my head. "Would you want to drive by my school?"

Bradley nods, exuberant. "I'd *love* to drive by your school."

"Yeah? Because then we'll have to rush with lunch—"

Bradley snorts. "Please! They don't want us to go back there anytime soon. Henry Charbonneau and his new man will probably lock up the store and have sex in the dressing room. Or the display window."

"This is me," I say, pointing to my car.

"Don't you mean to say, 'This is my car'?" Bradley says, employing the voice of slick car guy. "Or have you become one with your sedan?"

"I am the Taurus," I say.

Bradley nods. "I am the eggman." He gets in my car, ignoring my flurry of apologies for the trash on the floor, the overstuffed ashtray. He makes himself comfortable, one hand behind his head, and I realize how nice it is to have a passenger. If perchance I stopped breathing, he could take the wheel.

Bradley sighs. "Where are we off to? What school do you go to?"

And this leads me to think about tense-problems: Do I currently go to school there, or, or . . . what?

"Woodrow Wilson. But I'm not really going to school that much . . . ," I say.

Catherine Bennett, perpetual backseat driver, screams, *Because she doesn't know how to pay attention.*

"I wondered. Since this *is* a school day."

"I went to school the day before yesterday. Monday. But just in the morning."

There is a big old pregnant pause before Bradley cocks his head and says, "And so . . ."

And so I drive out of downtown, to the threaded blandness of the highway, almost missing my exit as I tell Bradley the story: I tell my sad story, of course I do, but I also tell Alecia Hardaway's story. Alecia Hardaway mainstreamed, Alecia Hardaway never, ever quite right. Alecia Hardaway surprisingly quite good at algebra, but bad at social equations. I tell Bradley the dark heart of the story, how Mrs. Bennett would throw out an obligatory request for everyone to *listen up* as she stood in front of the classroom, chalk in hand, how she would move in for the kill, her voice laced with awful happiness: "Alecia! Alecia, honey. What color are the Kleenex on my desk? What is your favorite kind of soup?"

And then came the horror of Alecia Hardaway's frantic blurting, her sweet pride: she can answer every question and damn it, she *will* answer every question. And, oh, how Mrs. Bennett would give such a benevolent smile: "Yes! The Kleenex are blue! I like chicken noodle soup too!"

I tell Bradley how Alecia Hardaway's face pinkened with the excitement of knowing every single question, of getting everything right, while the rest of the class laughed out their groans, their sickness, or stared at the floor, or sketched smiley faces in their spiral notebooks. I tell him how even people who seemed nominally nice acted jackassy: Evan Harper, the hot guy for the alternative girls, a long, cool drink nonpareil who writes righteous, rambling essays on varying social issues in Honors English, even Evan would laugh at Alecia Hardaway. Actually, he would chuckle sardonically, which was worse. And so I would sneak looks at his carved profile and rewrite the John Henry song:

> *Does your sense of justice only apply to fair-trade*
> *coffee beans, Evan Harper?*
> *Does your sense of justice only apply to supporting*
> *local coffee shops, Evan Harper?*
> *Your handsome face gets you many random fucks,*
> *and you want to slay Starbucks.*
> *Why must you laugh at a slow girl, Evan Harper?*

I tell Bradley how those moments had an otherworldly quality framed by the questions: Is this really happening and is it as bad as it seems? Why is Catherine Bennett's cruelty so bare and non-nuanced? So unpunished? Except for the spectacle of Mrs. Bennett's skirt ripping when she was freaking out on me. "That is biblical," Bradley says, pumping his fist.

I pour out my heart as I drive; it is a sweet relief. But there is one thing I do not tell Bradley. That day of

Mrs. Bennett's Kleenex and Chicken Soup Questionnaire was the day my mother was killed. I do not tell him the grotesque symmetry, the wildly unsubtle connection between cowardice—me, looking down, drawing migrating monarch butterflies on my homework while Mrs. Bennett grilled Alecia—and punishment: the car jumping the curb, my mother standing there on the corner that September morning, cappuccino in hand. She was on her morning break, heading back to work. I do not allow my mind to picture the impact, but I do allow for the snowy and cinnamoned peaks of her cappuccino to wobble and then slam into the side of her cup. Just that much.

I *do* tell Bradley about the Target horror show, about standing in the checkout lane on a Saturday morning at Target with my mom, discussing where we'd go for lunch: an unsuspecting bliss before the world imploded. My mother was complaining about the weather forecast—the August heat and saunalike humidity—not knowing, of course, that she would not live to see winter. But that Saturday morning she was fully alive and reaching for an Almond Joy, when there was the sudden bad luck of Alecia Hardaway and her mother getting in line behind us, of Alecia saying: "Hi, Sandinista! Hi, Sandinista! Hi, Sandi, you're a real cool person! You're a real cool person every day!"

I said a quick hello; I smiled lethargically and took a ferocious interest in the new fusion chewing gums—banana and mango cream, lime and strawberry. Soon I would be far away from the strange, slow girl who had seemingly memorized the name of every person who passed by her at

Woodrow Wilson High School. Usually students were nice to Alecia, but once I'd seen the cheerleaders mocking her aggressive friendliness in the halls, the cruelest Bob Whites circling behind Alecia and stage-whispering: "Hi, Craig! You're cool, Craig! Look, it's Lauren! Hi, Lauren!"

But right then it was all *Oh fuck me and double fuck my bad luck* because as it turned out, our moms knew each other, our moms had been in some lame Mommy and Me playgroup back in the day and appeared to have genuine affection for each other—Alecia's mom told my mom: "I remember you! You had purple hair! You were the other young mom in that group!"

And my own mom, so enthusiastic and kind: "Of course! I remember you, too. I haven't seen you in years. You look just the same! You haven't aged a bit!"

Oh, great, it was *on*, it was all *Welcome to Awkwardville: America's Hometown.* The subject turned, perilously, to Woodrow Wilson High School, and Alecia's mom proved her knowledge of our exemplary public school system by saying: "Alecia is getting on fine at Woodrow Wilson! Oh, it's sooo good for her to be with her *peers*, compared to when she was in the separate special ed classroom back in junior high."

Meanwhile, Alecia Hardaway kept kicking it with her wrenching chorus of "You're a real cool person, Sandinista, you're a real cool person every day," as if I had ever given her more than the random creeped-out smile in the hall. And so I made excruciating small talk: "Thanks, Alecia. You're cool, too. You're cool every day." Alecia's mother gave me a ravishing smile that made me suicidal, and said, "Alecia's going to be doing algebra on her own this year! She has shown a real affinity for math—so she's going to take algebra without her paraprofessional."

My own mother smiled at Alecia. It was a real smile, not some lame bullshit grin. "Alecia, that's terrific! Truthfully, I despise all forms of mathematics. I'm afraid Sandinista agrees with me. She's taking algebra this year too."

"With Mrs. Bennett?" Mrs. Hardaway asked me. Even then I knew Alecia's mom shouldn't be taking such a bright tone, for Mrs. Bennett was widely known to be insane.

"Yeah." I nodded, wishing myself away from the checkout lane and into the parking lot, into the car, into the wide, wide world.

And then Alecia's mother said it: "I hear she's tough but good!"

Alecia Hardaway had grown bored with the conversation and was looking at the Pokémon cards and candy. My mother and Mrs. Hardaway grinned at each other under the fluorescent lights as the elephant in the room—Target!—rose up and moonwalked through the cosmetics section before he Rollerbladed back to Kitchenware and juggled butcher knives in his brand-new SpongeBob underwear. Because, um, hello? Why in the name of Christ would Alecia's mother think it would be good for her to have a "tough" teacher? *Tough but good!*

Finally my own deluded mother paid for our trash bags and tampons and lip liners, and we made our escape.

I tell Bradley how Mr. and Mrs. Hardaway went to my mother's funeral, how Alecia sat between her parents in a sparkly black dress, interrupting the service with her blurted, pure-hearted interjections: "Sandinista looks sad. Mom, do you think Sandinista's sad?" I don't tell him that Mrs. Hardaway dropped off gorgeous food for me in the endless autumn weeks after my mother died: Caprese salads, bittersweet brownies swirled with cream cheese, eggplant lasagnas. I don't tell Bradley that Mrs. Hardaway left many messages on my machine, inviting me to dinner with her family, and that I never returned a single call. But I certainly gobbled up the meals—packed in thoughtful, disposable pans flanked by ice packs—she left on my front porch.

"Christ," Bradley says, rubbing his face. "It was nice of her family to go to your mom's funeral. God, September? Just four months ago?"

I shrug. "Yeah."

"Jesus. That's what I say to all of it: Jesus! Man, I hope I haven't been too bitchy about the Windex or anything," he says.

"You are a kind instructor in the art of Windexing." I say.

Bradley's voice is soft. "So, without your mom—"

"We were going to Europe next year. I mean, we were *going to go* to Europe next year. That was the plan. My mom wanted me to see the fashion capitals of Europe." I can feel tears coming, so I quickly say, "I know it's kind of lame to go to Europe with a parent." My mind cooks up the mean response: *Now you won't have to worry about that, little lady!*

Bradley smiles; his voice is tender. "It's not lame. I wish the two of you could have done that."

I start to feel queasy as I turn onto the exit ramp for Woodrow Wilson High School.

"Bradley, this is the gateway to hell."

"What would Woodrow Wilson say about all of this? Don't get me wrong, St. Matthew's sucked, too. But I mean, there you expect it to suck, you are following in the footsteps of Adam, as old St. Aquinas says."

I had no idea that old Saint Aquinas said that, which makes me thinks that at least the actual education is better if you go Catholic. Though I'm pretty surprised that Bradley went to the most exclusive high school in the city; I thought he was like me.

"You *expect* a little better treatment from a public school," Bradley says. "What with Big Brother watching and all. Maybe high school just sucks in general. College is a million times better: if you're gay, whatever, you can just sort of go ahead and be gay. At St. Matthew's? Not so much."

"I am highly honored to have a St. Matthew's alum in my car. Mr. Blazer and School Crest, I salute you. And I thought you might be Catholic"—I point to the crucified-Jesus tattoo on his thumb—"but I had no idea that you were some Catholic *fancy pants.*"

Bradley laughs. "Oh, well, absolutely I am a tattooed Catholic fancy pants. And that would not be a bad name for a blog: the Catholic Fancy Pants."

But Bradley's words zigzag into buzzy nothingness, because as soon as I turn into the school parking lot, I see it. Catherine Bennett is back. Her car is in its usual spot in the teachers' row, her WELL-BEHAVED WOMEN RARELY MAKE HISTORY! bumper sticker taunting me.

Bradley looks at me. "What is it?"

"She's back."

Did the school do nothing? Is that even possible? Legal?

"Are you kidding? Her ass should totally be fired. Man, I thought only the Catholics were this lame," Bradley says mournfully. He leans over the bucket seats and awkwardly puts his arm around my shoulder. I put the car in park and sit there, staring at Catherine Bennett's car.

Bradley sighs. "I mean, a normal person? Their skirt catches on the desk and comes down? A normal person would take the whole week off. For that alone." Bradley clears his throat. He is working very hard. "This is massively, massively fucked up. *Massively.*"

I stare out the window. I had thought waiting for the school to call made me stoic and mannered, a rawboned Midwesterner staring out at the frosty fields. *I shall bide my time.* Perhaps it was my rampant Midwesternitis that made me prim and polite, my Kansas City calling card: *I don't want to bother anybody! I'll go ahead and wait for you to call!* But probably geography has nothing to do with any of this; probably the school of We Will Mistreat You With Pleasure If You Let Us has an international open-admissions policy. And look at me: My mother gave me a punk-rock name, but my spirit is composed of elevator music: *Tra-la-la-la./Don't mind me./I'm a nice girl./I have good manners./I'll not bother you./Tra-la-LA!*

Because look how easy I have made it for the school; I have a bruise on my ribs from where my desk slammed into me when that crazy bitch freaked and kicked the desk leg and I have said nothing.

Still, isn't the school worried that I will contact an attorney? Do they not think I will report this to the state? Do they not think that I just might have a pretty pink and cream gun in my glove box?

But as I look at Woodrow Wilson High School, my rib starts to ache and pulse. Epiphany comes as soft sickness, acid pangs in the gut: the school knows of my personal situation, they know I am an eighteen-year-old with no parents. They know, a quick look at my transcripts, that I am not some shiny-haired Caitlin off to Yale, not someone whose name they would call out at graduation to a mad blast of applause. They have nothing in the world to fear from a girl like me: motherless, mediocre, my only As in art and English.

"Let's blow this Popsicle stand," Bradley says, his voice heavy with kindness, and so I drive off—there's not a reason in the world to stay.

Bradley seems to know that my brain has gone muzzy, possibly because when I merge onto the highway, a semi blows its horn. I always pass too close.

"For lunch we're getting burgers and fries and milk shakes, chica. We are having a comfort-food extravaganza and we are going to eat everything on our plates, even the wrappers, and you know what?" Bradley claps his hand on my knee and gives it a nice little shake. "We are going to love every last bite."

And so we do, we drive through and get burgers with bacon and cheese, and chicken strips, as if animal death is the antidote for all this—*Viva the slaughterhouse!*

But of course it does make us feel a little better, doesn't

it, and we eat in a deserted park, brushing the snow off an ancient wooden picnic table carved with inane graffiti: DO YOU GET HI? FOR A GOOD TIME CALL JULIE'S SEXY GRANDMA. I HEART TITS.

When we finish the winter picnic, we smoke our comfort—tobacco for me, weed for Bradley—and it's back to work we go, where all afternoon my mind flashes images of Catherine Bennett teaching algebra as if nothing ever happened, and I wonder, exactly, what the social expectation is: Is everyone expected to act like nothing happened? Like Monday was just another day in paradise?

And I am paying attention, I am paying attention, I know how to pay attention and I make change and I sell powder blue cashmere sweaters with iridescent pearl buttons, and men's black tuxedo pants with a charcoal stripe. I Swiffer the floor, I Windex the mirrors in the dressing room, I fill and refill the candy dishes, and I have the satisfaction of this, though occasionally I check my home messages—surprise, surprise, nobody has called. No one is curious about me. No one would like to see how I am doing; both nobody and no one would like to go for coffee.

Okay: I understand how unnuanced the whole situation is and I understand that people enjoy being helpful and prescriptive if your problem is singular and manageable. Boyfriend dump you? It's all: Been there, sister. Smoke and write your stricken poetry and you will feel better in approximately seven months. But the school thing on top of the dead-mom thing is too much, one melodrama too many, and a girl becomes Typhoid Mary of the Plains. This is my fault too. After my mom died, I routinely blew off my friends for such minor offenses: I remember a sympathy card with a peach rose photographed in soft focus like an aging starlet that infuriated me.

But now there is Bradley.

I see him crouch behind the rack of coats, pull his cell phone out of his jacket pocket, punch in numbers, and wait, his eyes cast down, his dark lashes fringing the planes of his cheekbones. He's waiting, too.

When he stands up, he gives me a bright smile that seems full of effort and says, "What's your plan for tonight, Sandinista?"

"Advil and vino?"

"Nice," he says. "I'm there."

And so he is. When we lock up for the night, when the minutiae of commerce are done—counting out the cash drawer, the soft shuffle of bills, the crisp flick and flutter of checks, the rusty *zi-i-ip* of the bank deposit bag—we drive to my house, cranking the radio and smoking, the feeling of a fun night on deck undercut with the specter of Catherine Bennett behind my eyelids. She might be popping a Lean Cuisine in the microwave right now, or watching *Law & Order* or ironing clothes for tomorrow, which is a school day, after all . . . heigh-ho, heigh-ho, it's off to work she goes!

But then there is the joy of scraping my key against the doorknob in the darkness. Can you guess who forgot to turn on the porch light this morning? Can you guess who isn't *paying attention*? There is the joy of having someone standing behind me, so that I can open the door without the fear of a stalker jumping out of the snowy hedges and pushing me into my house. I get the door open, and first thing I do is look at the answering machine, at the red zero flashing in the darkness: molten, taunting. But then Bradley follows me inside. When I flip on the light, he doesn't do the jackassy thing where a first-time visitor looks around your home like they're at a museum, eyes flitting and voice buoyant: *I love the red paint! Did you make that vase? What a super print, I didn't know you liked Marc Chagall. And the framed album cover of* Sandinista! *Très apropos! Oh, we bought that bookshelf at Ikea too. We painted ours a glossy apple green.*

There's just Bradley being himself, smiling, his shoulders slightly hunched, his hands in his pockets. He stands like that for a moment before he takes his coat off, slings it on the arm of the couch, and says, "I love it here, Sandinista. I'm never leaving."

But he is, of course. He'll leave us all in two weeks when he goes back to college, the semester break a shocking six weeks, but I try to push this reality from my thoughts and enjoy having Bradley at my house.

I haven't had a boy spend the night since the whole debacle with Jonathan H. last summer. Jonathan spent the night on the Fourth of July when my mother went to visit her friend Arla in Omaha. Oh, the embittered drama of last summer now seems swathed in cotton candy, lit by pink and lavender incandescent bulbs. Had I known what the future held, I would have cherished the innocence of smashed romance and written bland odes celebrating my generic teenage heartache. I would have blessed Jonathan for dumping me for Tatiana Turner, she of the porn-star alliteration name and the extensive body piercings. Through her whorishly tight T-shirt, you could see the flat silver hoops that ringed her pierced nipples, two perky Saturns that Jonathan could not, apparently, resist.

But Bradley is no Jonathan. Bradley sits on the couch and pulls out his cell phone to check his messages. My soul mate. It seems as if he as always been here, not in a ceramic-elf-on-a-shelf way, but in the way of naturalness, of inevitability. And so our angsty slumber party commences: I order pizza without the fear that the Pizza Hut delivery man will peer inside, see me alone, and show up after his shift with complimentary breadsticks and an ice pick.

We eat a shitload of pizza. We watch TV and we smoke and we drink diet soda. We get in my bed together, some Ricky and Lucy high jinks concerning this: many, many jokes about keeping one foot on the floor and pledges about not taking advantage of one another. I'm still a little buzzed from the caffeine when I hear Bradley's breath begin to rise and fall evenly. Just when I think he's dead asleep, Bradley gets out of bed. I listen to the squeak of his footsteps on the pine-plank hallway. The thick 1970s carpet muffles sound in the rest of the house—we had thought of pulling it up, but in the end we just went ahead and stayed with the toxic shag. So I don't hear anything at all before there is the aggressive jiggling of the sliding glass door.

Next, Bradley checks the steel locks on the front door—*click click click click*—and then I hear his footsteps coming down the hallway again, and he gets back into bed. I have the far-off thought that he will make a good father someday.

Soon, Bradley really is asleep. But my mind is full of parking lots and Alecia Hardaway and the pleasure of having someone in bed next to me. Bradley must use a fruited shampoo, because curled up under the blankets he smells warm, citrusy. I have a sudden sensory memory of an orange Christmas cake my mother used to make. Orange peels next to a blue bowl, ribbons of batter falling from the electric hand beater. And Catherine Bennett. Of course she's there too. Catherine Bennett, Catherine Bennett. I look at the clock on the nightstand: 2:30.

Quietly, I creep out of bed and tiptoe out of my room. In the hall mirror, I wipe the sad-clown mascara smears from beneath my eyes, put my coat on and head into the night: the cold car, the choking ignition, the icy air on my face. It's only because I have someone waiting for me at home that I have the courage to leave the house at this hour. Hear me now, O rapists and muggers and frantic meth heads who will tap my car window at any given intersection: Bradley awaits.

I take the MapQuest directions out of my purse and let the car warm in the driveway while I study my path. And then I light a cigarette, switch on my headlights and drive slowly and carefully through the side streets of my neighborhood.

I speed up as I drive on and on into the heart of the cold and starless night, thinking, *Oh, Catherine Bennett, I am coming for you,* a nervous pioneer exploring the far-flung suburbs with their replicating tanning salons and Burger Kings and Kwik Shops. When the street names start to sound like cowboy movies, I know I'm getting warm. Here is Trailblazer Avenue, here is Cattleman Court, here is Maverick Lane. And here is my right turn, Ponderosa Lane, where shaggy pine trees in the front yards dwarf all the ranch houses. With my heart racing and all my stalkerina impulses on fire, I squint at the passing house numbers illuminated by porch lights. I'm expecting revelation, something along the lines of the humiliation and the exaltation and Christ only knows what. When I reach the 1100 block of Ponderosa Lane, I slow down, my foot taking a soft turn on the brake, and there it is, 1207 Ponderosa Lane.

Catherine Bennett lives in a cranberry-colored ranch house with a maple door and shutters. Though it's the first week of January, there's still a life-sized wooden toy soldier—or is it a fucking *nutcracker?*—with painted rose-pink cheeks, a modest smile and a tall black hat garlanded with green and red Christmas tinsel.

I think: *Why would a woman so efficient and mathematical not have taken down her Christmas decorations?*

The front is dark, though there is a lit window at the side of the house, a golden rectangle cheering the side yard. Still, as I drive on, inch by inch past her house, there is a pallor here that I recognize. Catherine Bennett's house has the same doomed *whose woods these are/I think I know* vibe of my own house. I imagine that Catherine Bennett is in her bedroom. Catherine Bennett is watching a crime show. Maybe Catherine Bennett is dead. Perhaps she slipped on the shower floor and her body is decomposing, because of course there's nobody to call the ambulance, the morgue, whatever. Of course there's no one to help her, because she's all alone, isn't she?

I crack my window and throw out my cigarette butt. I

immediately light up another, the match sparking blue in the darkness. I must consider that Catherine Bennett might not be home at all. Catherine Bennett might be on some grief-limned vacation. With her affinity for paying attention, her expertise at forethought, she's surely bought that special device that I keep meaning to buy, the one that I really, really need, the device that allows lights to click on every night at the same time, a device that makes each and every burglar put finger pensively to chin and think, *What light in yonder window breaks? Ah, it must be that the home-owner is inside. Alas, I shall try another house.*

But why would I fear someone who merely wants to steal a TV when I am not in my house? So maybe that's not the device I want at all; what I want is the opposite thing, a shield to blacken the house and make it appear that no one is home so that all the big guns—the rapists and killers—will leave me be and move on to a well-lit house of prey.

I circle the block so I can drive past Catherine Bennett's house again, and if I were a person of substance or bravery I would certainly do *something.* I would perhaps get out of my car and rush the creepy toy soldier/nutcracker; I would fly into him and knock him on his faux-oak ass.

Instead I park on the street directly in front of Catherine Bennett's house: *Guess who's here! Catherine Bennett, what light through yonder window breaks? Oh, that's right, it's me. In your words,* a girl who will not need algebra if she's just going to get married and have babies. *But let's say I'm not going to get married and have babies. In truth, Mrs. Bennett, I am not even dating anyone, so that's not really on the horizon. Let's also say, for the sake of argument, that I'm not going off to college, either. Let's say that without my mother, without our doomed year in Europe, I am completely without a plan. Perhaps I should listen to your colleague Lisa Kaplansky and start applying for grants and loans and scholarships to study art or literature. I shall steer clear of mathematics, Mrs. Bennett! But really? I cannot envision myself living in a dorm with a roommate who drinks herself sick on keg beer every night—some random Caitlin or Anna so glad to be away from her parents' prying eyes!*

Hey, Catherine Bennett, do you think what the counselors say is true: that people without a plan are more likely to act upon their impulses? And the night rises up around me, harsh and black-velvet cold, as I smoke and look at Mrs. Bennett's house.

I get my gun out of my glove box; I get out of my car.

I close the car door very quietly, as if trying not to wake a sleeping baby, I randomly coo: "Shhh."

The street is sugared with snow and grit and so I move carefully. I hold my gun up in my coat sleeve and walk, a girl with no hands, across the street. I really should be used to the cold by now.

I step from the street up to the curb, and then I crunch across the front lawn, each step shattering the ice, a crashing storm-trooper stomp that ruins the snowy silence. In a lame movie, a soft-eyed deer would appear leaping under the streetlights—a moment of foreshadowing and throwaway majesty—but in real life there's just the gigantic nutcracker standing sentry in the front yard. And I hadn't seen it from the street, but the side yard features more holiday art: an ancient wooden Santa whose red coat is surely flaking lead paint, waving from his sad sled—a pioneer's wooden cart full of faded boxes. Santa's hand waves jovially at nobody. In my own hand, the gun feels like it has adhered to my fingers, like I have an all-new metal palm, because my gloves are mostly for aesthetic purposes—soft navy suede lined with a sateen fabric that makes my fingers feels colder than if I were wearing no gloves at all.

Earlier, on the radio news, I learned that it's official: today is the coldest day since 1987. I flare my nostrils so my snot won't freeze, and when my eyes water, my mascaraed lashes freeze in chunks: my new world is fringed in icy black glitter. It is so quiet that when I hear panting, I expect to turn and see some rottweiller snow monster, icicles dangling from its gaping jaws. But the sound is just me, breathing.

I crunch through the snow to the side of the house, to the lit window. And I thrill a little—my heart hammering in my chest—Catherine Bennett has no idea that I am standing outside her house with a gun. Who's not paying attention now? I press my back to the cold house for a moment and then, step by snow-crashing step, I slither down the side of the house, closer to the window, my gun tucked up in my coat sleeve but there all the same, bumping along the cold siding of Catherine Bennett's house. *Mrs. Bennett! Yoo-hoo! Do you know who's standing outside your house right now! Are you paying attention? Do you even know how to pay attention?*

At the window frame, I lean forward. There are icicles over my head, some sort of icy horror-show premonition. The window is curtainless, though fogged, perhaps just above the heat vent. I put my hand on the side of the wooden frame, press my body closer and take a look inside.

Gazing though the fogged pane gives me baby kitten eyes, the world wreathed in gauze, but I can see Catherine Bennett. I can see Catherine Bennett sitting on a turquoise couch.

I am holding my breath so I don't hear the monster dog panting. When I finally exhale, my breath is a slow plume that defogs a few inches of the window.

Turquoise.

The turquoise couch looks to be velvety, with a baroque arched maple back. I had envisioned Mrs. Bennett as someone with a drab, neutral couch, nubby and office-beige and possibly sheathed in a vinyl couch condom. I had not imagined her drawn to the fanciful. Or had I? "Alecia, what kind of earrings are those, goodness gracious. Pull back your hair and let me see. . . . Oh, ponies . . . , no, unicorns . . . sparkly purple unicorns."

There is a poster-sized photograph of Mrs. Bennett and a man, Mr. Bennett, I'm guessing, on the wall. Catherine Bennett is eating an ice cream bar. She's looking right back at me, as if in a trance. But no, no, she's not looking *at* me, but just below me, at the TV. The voices are muted, metallic. My head cocked at an angle must look large, floating and tilted. I step forward and trip on something,

I exhale a snow-star sound, the softest *fuuuuuhhck*.

I look down and see that beneath the windowsill are two stone lawn ornaments. The angle of the gutters has protected them from a crush of snow. I imagine they get plonked with the occasional icicle. I crouch down—my cold gun at my knee—and see that they are the granite frog and toad from the Frog and Toad books. The soft light from the living room window illuminates their familiar faces: Toad is reading a small stone book; Frog holds one amphibious finger pensively to his lip.

Alecia, what kind of animal is a unicorn?

Alecia, where would a unicorn be found? A zoo? In the wild?

The air is shaded blue from the cold, my wild roaring breath in my ears and my mother's voice in my head, her pseudo psychiatrist voice that annoyed me: *Do not turn your depression inward. This is what women do. I'm not being sexist, Sandinista, it's a statistical fact. When you're sad, baby, man up.*

I look in at Mrs. Bennett, a sad lumpen toad in a lavender sweat suit. She has the hard-glazed look of someone using TV like gin: a little something to take the edge off when she's home by herself.

I take in a sharp breath that tingles my sore rib.

Alecia, hey, sleepyhead!

Something on TV makes Mrs. Bennett laugh out loud.

I pick up Toad and I take a few steps back and feel a little like Lady Liberty, like the things I am holding are equally weighted, gun in one hand, yard art inspired by children's literature in the other. I step back, taking aim.

And there's no deciding, of course I'm not going to . . . of course the gun is a prop. But if I did do it, everyone would understand. Surely my fellow students at Woodrow Wilson High School would remember Alecia's face, first looking out the window with a dreamland expression, her world locked away, but then . . . A deep inhale and my teeth sting from the cold as I remember, as I try not to exhale, Mrs. Bennett tiptoeing behind her, splaying her fingers out next to her mouth before leaning down next to Alecia and yelling *"Boo!"* Alecia gripping the soft roll of her turtleneck sweater with both hands; Alecia letting out a hurt-bird "Whaaaaaat?"

With an awkward underhanded lob, I throw Toad at Catherine Bennett's lit window.

I expect the sweetly lacquered crescendo of glass crashing on snow. But there is only a large thud, then a slow, sharp sound of a crack in the pane. I'm off and not turning back, the snow making my sprint quicksand slow, and then my heart slamming away as I slip-slide across the street to the safety of my car, the chilling second of *Oh my God where are my keys,* but there they are, right in the ignition, and I get into my car and drive out of Catherine Bennett's subdivision with the calm assurance of a suburban mom, a firefighter, a beefy police officer.

As I'm exiting onto the interstate there is the satisfaction of the sirens in the distance, soft, swirling, pleading: *Alecia, Alecia. Alecia . . .*

I crank up the Clash all the way home, my adrenaline harnessed in perfect pitch. My gun is on the passenger seat and I am Sandinista Jones, motherfuckers, all the way home.

* * *

I let myself into my house quietly, and from the living room I can hear already Bradley snoring. He has slept through this little adventure. I have the feeling of the wife home from meeting the lover, sneaking in quietly next to my sweet cuckold of a husband: *Night, honey!* His snoring is loud as a French horn, it even has a golden brassy undertone; I look forward to the day I know him well enough to tease him about this.

I will myself not to sleep so I can enjoy all the scenarios racing though my mind, how Catherine Bennett might say: *Officer, I was just sitting here watching TV, minding my own darn business, isn't that the way, and then Toad sailed through the window, and I could have been killed if it hit me at just the right angle in my temple, and oh, Officer, please can you try to find my potential assailant, and please can you charge them with attempted homicide, and I bought Frog and Toad at a yard sale in 1990 and how will I ever find another Toad? Oh, Officer, my husband, Rupert, is dead, and who will protect a lamb like me? And just think of poor old Frog in the side yard by himself— why, he's just like me: I have become one with Frog.* Then, later, Catherine Bennett duct-taping plastic wrap over her window and having a private pity party: *Kids these days! And after everything I do for them.*

So I can enjoy Bradley next to me, I fight the dragons of coziness, my mind abuzz with drama, with faux-rap-star dialogue: *Bitch, be glad it was the freaky stone toad and not the gun.* I think: *Who am I? Who am I? Who am I?* And then, sleep.

THURSDAY
CONSIDER THE CAKES

Morning has broken like the first morning and all that, but I try not to be happy about Bradley in bed next to me; I try to accept and surrender to a bitter brand of dirty-nursing-home loneliness. I do not want to be bamboozled by flashes of happiness; I must be inured to the world, I must accept the here and now so that I am not perpetually shocked that my mother is never here to snuggle my back, to vex me with a cheery "Fie, slugabed!"

Still, I feel some small satisfaction as I think of Catherine Bennett's broken window, of some tired rookie officer dispatched to her lonely ranch house, how he will go home to his house, kiss his wife and children and be grateful for the bounty that is his life. And I feel the fluted edge of joy as I look over at Bradley, who, like a celibate bridegroom, sleeps on top of the covers in his T-shirt and jeans. His slate-colored oxford shirt is folded carefully on the chair next to the bed; his shoes are lined up next to my bedroom door. Tucked around his shoulders is the red and black quilt my mother made out of an old Halloween ladybug costume. He snores lightly now, the French horn packed away. It seems as if he snores *thoughtfully,* actually, a certain shushing *Masterpiece Theatre yes yes yes I see yes yes yes yes* as his breath rises and falls.

It is eight-thirty. My fourth day out. Usually, if your mom—or you—doesn't phone in your absence by noon the school secretary will call, scolding and grinchy: *Could we all be a little more considerate? Could we all remember that the teachers need time to fill out missing assignment sheets?* But I guess no one is really all that concerned about the timely completion of my biology homework. I guess the jig is pretty much up.

"Doctor," Bradley shouts, his eyes closed. He flails his hands around, chopping up dust motes over his head. The wild dust is lit by the sun shining between the pulled shade and the window. Before he says anything else, the dust shimmies and re-forms into the same glittering gray plank.

"Doctor, I was dreaming that I woke up next to a beautiful woman in a room that smelled of lavender."

This makes my throat catch. The embroidered sachets in my underwear drawer were made by my mother—squares from old pillowcases stuffed with organic lavender and stitched up. She made a big deal of the fact that her sachets were all-organic. As if I were going to eat them or smoke them.

"Doctor," Bradley says softly, opening his eyes wide, and grimacing at me in mock horror. "I had all my clothes on, so I can't say for sure: I think—Mother of God, don't let it be true!—I think . . . she may have taken advantage of me!"

And so he gives any potential awkwardness the boot and the day starts with laughter. And I think how nice it was to spend the night with a boy when we were both fully clothed. Given both the physical and mental residual weirdness of sex, the Buddy Overnight is far superior. Even leaving out the Science-Fair-from-Hell freak-show quality of sex, there is a calm and certain purity in doing things this way. Maybe the monks have it right.

Bradley and I get out of bed together and say "Mornin', honey!" as if we are asswipes in a Kellogg's commercial. And he doesn't gawk at my room: not at the dust that settles over everything like sugar snow, or the posters or the photographs pinned here and there, or the framed cross-stitch sampler on the wall. He merely asks if he can take a shower.

But then the peace of Christ or whomever flies the coop and I worry about the football stadium–quality cleanliness of the bathroom. I haven't really done much scrubbing since my mother died, and not before then, either. My mother did most of the household chores while I watched TV or wrote in my journal or Web-stalked boys who had done any minor thing to interest me: Matt MacGregor's sublime research paper on F. Scott Fitzgerald led me on a fruitless Google journey that ended at his aunt Amy's Facebook page, filled with status updates about her miniature dachshunds.

While Bradley showers, I wash out a cereal bowl that has been in the dishwasher for days, for weeks, Cocoa Krispies turned to chocolate pebbles with papier-mâché. I put English muffins on the counter with a jar of peanut butter, a jar of honey that I did not buy. The unheralded world of groceries is my own little BC and AD: I think of how the jar of honey was once in my mother's palm at the farmers' market: *Oh, honey, yes, I think we need honey. Sandinista loves honey on her toast.* I open the cabinet a final time to check for any other breakfast delicacies for Bradley. I stare at the Trappist jam for a moment—there's just a skin of red fruit left at the bottom of the mason jar—and think of my mother spooning it on her sourdough toast. I take it out and put it next to the jar of honey. The digital clock on the microwave oven says 9:13. If I were at school, I would be in Mrs. Bennett's class.

I hope Alecia Hardaway has the flu. I will her to have some mild bug, visualizing her on the family-room couch eating toast and watching cartoons, her nice mother puttering around in the kitchen. I shower while Bradley eats breakfast. I keep the water as boiling hot as I can stand it, so that my skin is roasting, porcine. When I step out of the shower, I towel off the fogged mirror and look at my body. I can count all my ribs.

And the bruise on my ribs where my desk slammed against me is changing colors: it's not so dark now, the outline of Italy is fading into a greenish, blurred boot.

When I look out the bathroom window, I see that Bradley

has gone into the backyard to smoke. He's also checking his cell phone and looking up at the sky carefully, as if praying or searching for spacecraft. I study him until it feels bad, like I'm spying, and then I blow-dry my hair.

* * *

I drive Bradley to work, and when he gets out of the car, he offers up a guttural "Baby, that was terrific. I'll give you a call sometime." And so there is more laughter and the day lights up, clear sunshine and still some snow on the ground, the air fresh as spearmint. But the second he's gone into the Pale Circus—why did Henry Charbonneau give me a day off, the last thing I need is a day off—and I'm idling in my car on Thirty-Eighth Street, I start feeling my feelings, as my mother always advised me to do.

My feelings are not so hot.

My feelings are that Catherine Bennett has won at some crazy game that I didn't realize I was going to have to play. My feelings are that a granite toad tossed through a window is a lame-ass gesture that barely constitutes revenge. My feelings are that Jesus himself would not be all turn-the-other-cheek–esque about Catherine Bennett, that he'd kick it like: *Whatsoever you do to the least of my brothers, that you do unto me, so don't be so lame and let Alecia Hardaway s-u-u-ffer. . . .*

I cannot shake this off.

But what else is there to do except drive home with these bad feelings and attend to the business of the day?

Back at home, I do the breakfast dishes. I cannot remember to buy the soap pellets or the little liquid gel-packs for the dishwasher, so I take all the dishes out of the dishwasher and wash them campfire-style, sans stars, sans s'mores, just water and the pan and the bubbles. I sweep the kitchen floor and come away with dustpans full of fluff and detritus. I scrape the last of the Trappist jam out of the jar with a spoon and slam it into the trash. I eat an Almond Joy.

I find my social security check in an avalanche of mail and then drive to Target, where I cash it at the in-store bank and buy tampons, dental floss, toothpaste, Monistat for my recurring yeast infection, and toilet paper: all the products that used to magically appear on the bathroom shelves. Well, what had I thought? That tampons were a perpetually replicating species, packed cotton peeking out from the slit end of the plastic applicator, coquettish and looking for a suitable mate?

While driving back home I realize I have forgotten my cell phone at Target. Of course I have, because I'm *not paying attention*. This could be far worse; I could have left, say, my *gun* at Target, resting on a display of Brawny paper towels. But no, it's safely tucked away in my glove box and of course I didn't take the gun in the store with me, but attention deficit disorder makes all things possible and I make a mental note to be careful about where I take it, where I leave it. (The gun isn't loaded, of course—I have no idea how to insert the bullets.) And so then I drive back and customer service does have my phone, some kind soul has turned it in, and so I'm a little buzzed on the good luck of that, but I come home to no new messages on my machine.

I stand in the living room holding my Target bags, reeling from no call no love no nada zilcherino from the school. I'm wondering how much longer I will be able to take my mother's absence and my chest feels like it is stuffed with bricks.

I turn on the computer and I surf the Web and I crank up one of my mom's old Clash CDs and do some deep breathing exercises. But I really can't take the house—the silence, the sadness—shriveled aloe plants in their terra cotta pots and ancient postcards on the fridge—GUINNESS IS GOOD FOR YOU, a rueful Jack Kerouac cradling a black and white cat, Carson McCullers with her sad eyes and fetching bob. Mostly the silence of the phone means that I am *out* of here.

*　*　*

I work out some hippie philosophy: I will know where I'm going once I get there. I avoid the school—a feat that takes some kind of Zen-master stoicism—and I drive downtown.

I cruise aimlessly.

I am Miss Global Warming! Instead of a sash and crown, I will wear a clever smokestack beret and string empty gas cans into an avant-garde necklace. Because I crave motion: I need forward motion. When I drive down Thirty-Eighth Street I am both relieved and embarrassed to see Bradley beneath the striped awning, inscrutable behind his vintage Ray-Bans. When he sees me, he breaks into a huge goofy smile. He walks out to meet me as I slow down and lower the passenger window.

"Sandinista!" He takes off his shades and squats down by the car door so we are eye level. "What are you doing here? Do you need some booze or chocolate?"

"I need neither booze nor chocolate, young man," I say, my voice dramatic as that of a 1940s heroine in a trim wool suit.

Bradley smiles. He points to St. Joseph's at the end of the street. "Do you have a boyfriend at the monastery? Or do you have some business at the pawnshop?" Bradley slips into a *Deliverance* accent. "Are you downtown fixing to pawn wedding rings to get ole Billy Joe John Jerry out of jail?"

"No, no, none of that. I'm checking up on you. Once a boy spends the night with me I turn into a total psycho stalker. Word to the wise."

Bradley smiles at an invisible TV camera somewhere in the distance, and in the jangly bass of a game-show host he says, "You'll always remember your first stalker: the letters, the calls, the restraining orders, the inevitable purchase of pepper spray and a pistol." He leans closer, resumes his regular voice. "Hey, are you okay?"

"Oh, I'm good. I just had some errands to run, and so, you know . . ."

A glimmering black Cadillac Escalade pulls up in front of the Pale Circus. Three boys wearing black wool capes, dark lipstick and nail polish swoop out of the car.

Bradley smiles. "And I'm off to battle the suburban goths."

"Word to Count Dracula," I say.

As I pull away, he gives the trunk of my car a pat and

heads back into the Pale Circus. I close the window and crank up the heat. As I'm lighting a cigarette I hear rap music, loud as sirens, flooding the street, and then a Volvo wagon parks in front of Erika's Erotic Confections. Two white college-age guys get out of the car, trailed by the sounds of Common and Kanye West: *I got two kids and my baby mama late, uh-oh, uh-oh, uh-oh.* They go into Erika's Erotic Confections, the car engine still running, the song still pumping—*I did what I had to did cuz I had the kid, uh-oh, uh-oh, uh-oh.*

I cruise around the block. My cigarette is not even smoked halfway down when the guys walk out of the shop with a large rectangular white bakery box tied with peppermint-striped ribbon. They are laughing and jostling around so much that I have the visual image of the warning sign at every swimming pool, even the bold black letters, the no-nonsense exclamation point: NO HORSEPLAY! But the cake is not dropped. They gently set it in the back of the wagon and exchange a high five. Then a fist bump. The hems of their long wool coats swing out and kiss as they turn away from each other and get back into the front seat. There's the rev of the engine—in the Volvo it comes out as a controlled keening: *ohhh, ohhh, ohhh*—and they're off.

I crush out my cigarette in the ashtray and enjoy the after-effect: brisk nicotine air in the safety of my car. And then because I don't have anywhere else to go and I'm a little hungry for something sweet I decide to brave it: I park my car and make my own trip to Erika's Erotic Confections. The door is galvanized steel with an ominous peephole at eye level. But inside, the walls are painted a deep mango, the floors tiled in black and white squares like a tropical soda shoppe. The air smells sweetly of batter, but beneath it a chemical note: the smell of industrial cleanser, of freshly mopped hospital floors. And from behind the counter: Erika. Her Cloroxed flattop has grown into a bob, colored to a bright cherry cola. She wears false eyelashes and an emerald on a sliver hoop strung through her left nostril.

"Hey there, *you,*" she calls out, as if genuinely happy to see me.

Me?

"Oh, hey," I say.

Erika stands at a long wooden table, surrounded by pastry bags, bowls of frosting and a huge cake.

"How's it goin'?" She has a pastry bag in hand, its metal tip sprouting a flourish of sea-foam-green icing.

"Not too bad, not too bad at all," I say, my voice bizarre with exaggerated casualness. Going closer, my heels striking the pretty tile like a teacup poodle tap tap tapping across the room, I can see what Erika is working on: a cake of a nude woman who has the body of a *Playboy* centerfold.

"I'll be with you in just one second." Erika squints and puts both hands around the pastry bag.

At first I think she's frosting ankle socks on the naked cake. But really, my eyes adjusting as if to bright sunshine, I see now that Erika is icing on a pair of sea-foam-green panties pulled down to the cake's ankles.

Jesus, I think, *what company makes that cake pan?* I feel my face warm and redden and know that I am the lamest of the lame: a cake is making me blush.

"There." Erika puts the pastry bag down. "Can I help you, hon?"

Her tone is sweet, as if she knows I am not here to gawk at the erect marzipan penis standing sentry next to the cash register, nor to flip through the photo album of graphic gateaux on the counter.

"Um . . . well, I'm just looking around a little."

"You *are*?" Erika widens her eyes and smiles.

"Well, I had a chocolate from here one time . . . it was really excellent."

"Oh! Thanks for telling me."

I try to train my eyes away from the marzipan penis, but Erika sees me stealing a quick look.

"My next project is to make a marzipan penis that ejaculates *money*."

I snort out a real laugh. "Coins or bills?"

Erika smiles. "The fountain effect of gold coins showering down would be pleasing, but rolled bills would be easier, architecturally.

"I'm Erika." She holds out her hand, and we shake. I don't know why I'm surprised that she has a mother's hand, a palm with the flaking roughness of someone who washes dishes.

"I'm Sandinista."

Erika nods, resolute. "Well, of course you are. Sandinista! Who else would you ever be?" She stares off for a moment. "God, that's a good album: *Sandinista!*"

She walks to the front cooler and pulls out a tray of triangular dark chocolates dusted with a yellow veneer of crystal sugar. "Names are funny, right? How they reveal a thing or two about your lineage? I have a friend named Flannery. Are her parents retired English professors?" Erika smacks one hand to her forehead, feigning shock. "Why, yes, they are."

She holds out the tray.

"Oh, they're so gorgeous!"

"Banana curry robed in fair-trade Venezuelan chocolate." Erika rolls her eyes. "I'm working on my website. Trying to stop whoring myself out with the tittie cakes. Try one! On the house."

"Thanks," I say. I pop one in my mouth and it's warm and sweet and savory, comforting but also interesting, like you hope the world will be.

"Wow . . . my God . . . these . . . are . . . just . . ." I tear up a little, thinking of my mother telling me how we would eat nothing but chocolate when we traveled through Switzerland on our big trip: *Fondues! Ingots! Bricks and bars of chocolate!* We would drink only chocolate, too: hot, with shots of espresso.

"Thanks." Erika gives me a curious, concerned look, and then walks behind the counter with the tray, takes three chocolates from the plate and arranges them in a little white bakery box. She bothers to tie it up with a peppermint-striped ribbon before handing it to me.

As I reach for my purse, Erika makes a disgusted click sound with her tongue. *Cllllllk!* "Jesus, I can't really expect you to pay for something you didn't ask for, Miss Sandinista."

And I'm thinking how that's not always the case, when she says, "My treat. You work at the Pale Circus, right?"

"Yes. I'm new."

She smiles. "I know. I saw you filling out your job application on the bench Monday morning. And smoking under the awning with Bradley on Tuesday. You went into Arne's shop after work that day. Wednesday, Henry Charbonneau came into work; you and Bradley went to lunch."

"You're right!"

And then she reads my mind.

"No, I'm not a stalker. Most people just come to Thirty-Eighth Street for liquor, porno sweets, pawned jewelry, pretty vintage clothes, jam, or Jesus. So a new person taking a job on this street is pretty notable here."

"Sure!"

She smiles. "I sort of work at the Pale Circus, too. As their chocolatier. Henry gave me my first order back when I opened up a few years ago."

"Of course! The candy next to the cash register. Your chocolates are so gorgeous. . . . They don't last long. People are so delighted by them."

"Thanks. They're all-organic. I usually bring them in first thing every morning. I don't make the circus peanuts. Henry buys them by the case at Costco. Cheap bastard." She winks at me and picks up her pastry bag. "Back to work!"

"Thanks so much for the candy." I turn to leave and notice that Erika sells the jams from the monastery. There they

are in a pyramid on the counter, achingly red jams and jellies in mason jars: chokecherry, raspberry, bumbleberry
and strawberry. Their gift tags display a crucified Jesus and
the words LOVE AND PRAYERS TO YOU FROM YOUR FRIENDS AT ST.
JOSEPH'S MONASTERY. Next to the jams is a display of chocolate
breasts. *Juxtaposition,* I think, my brain pleased to have
floated out a fat, smart word, but shouldn't I be in school
learning some others?

I wave good-bye to Erika, but when I have one hand on
the door, she waves me back in.

"One more thing." She cocks her head and squints down
at the cake, the rows of perfect sea-foam rosettes that create
the pulled-down panties.

"Isn't this absurd, Sandinista?" She waves her hands
over the cake, the large vanilla breasts, and the frosted pink
nipples as big as mini-muffins. "What passes for high
humor at the frat parties these days. Hoo-hoo-hoo! So
funny."

I nod, sympathetic—*Right?*—as if I have ever been to a
fraternity or bachelor party, as if I am some feminist sister
in the know.

Erika is squinting her eyes, as if observing me from a
great distance. "Want to see something, Sandinista?"

Uh-oh. Right away I can tell I do not want to see anything
at all. I'm no fan of the awkward social encounter, but what
can I do?

And so my own big smile is pure propriety, as is my star-
ling chirp: "I sure would!"

Erika reaches to a shelf underneath the table and pulls

out a can of Comet. She shakes the cleanser over a bowl of frosting next to the cake. Nothing. She frowns, and then pats the can with her palm. A cloud of dust puffs out, and then granules of pale green cleanser shower into the bowl. Erika coughs. And next there is the comforting whirr of the hand mixer, the seconds where talking would be futile. *Uh-oh.* When she turns off the mixer, she tilts the bowl so I can see: the frosting has turned a more saturated shade of pale seafoam green.

"Wow," I say.

She smiles. "Cool, right?"

I match her brightness: "Well . . . *yeah!* Very!"

"I use a shitload of Splenda in the frosting; it covers any taste. Artificial sweeteners are pure magic. Though they might give us cancer. Just use sugar in your coffee drinks if you like them sweet, okay?"

I nod. "That's what I use. Just sugar."

Her brow furrows while she works, whipping a spatula through the frosting. I'm thinking that the Comet might be a more immediate concern than the whole, um, cancer thing. Erica seems pretty crazy, but what's a gal to do, what's a gal to do. I know not. I can pay attention and that's it, that's all I can do. . . . I can study Erika and her poisoned icing until Catherine Bennett floats into the shop, shouting, *What does this cake taste like to you, Alecia? What flavor is in the cake? Yoo-hoo, Alecia! Are you paying attention?*

"I do this by hand, I don't use the Mixmaster," Erika says. She looks at the frosting, frowns, and squirts in some bright green food coloring. "Because if you use too much

Comet it bleaches the frosting out when you whip it. It goes from nice green to sickly pale green."

Psycho Martha Stewart sprinkles a bit more Comet into the frosting and I'm thinking, *Wouldn't that make it . . . kind of gritty,* when she scoops shortening out of a tub and turns the hand mixer on again.

It's all very migraine-licious, so I lift my hand to wave—see ya!—but Erika switches off the mixer and gives me a conspiratorial smile.

"When the jackass guys get sick, they never ever think it's the cake. They don't consider the cake! They assume it's the booze." She affects a baritone: "Dude, I got so wasted last night. I drank seventeen Jägermeister bombs, and then—dude!—I fucked the stripper, and then I threw up for five days. Ha!"

I chuckle along with Erika, but maybe she can tell what I'm thinking yet again because she says:

"Hey, don't flush your chocolates down the john, Sandinista! I worked hard on those. They are the cleanest food you could hope to eat. I only add my secret ingredients to food that exploits women!"

I laugh barkingly hard, as if the exploitation of women is nothing short of distilled hilarity.

She raises one pierced eyebrow at me. "I'm serious, Sandinista. Cake can be a form of social justice. The brothers we share the block with?" She nods in the direction of the monastery. "They would tell me to turn the other cheek, but sometimes a lady needs to turn the tables instead."

I am too flummoxed to think of any socially relevant

comment, so I thank her for the chocolates and hightail it out of the shop, taking a final look at the display of chocolate breasts: gentlemen, beware.

*　*　*

And then it's home again, home again, jiggety jog. It's me walking in the front door and seeing the ghost of my mother in my peripheral vision. She wears a sort of pith helmet and khaki pantsuit, as if she has not only risen from the dead but is now a minor character in a manly man Hemingway novel. She says: *Sandinista, sweet girl, please put your keys in the dish so that you don't have to go on ye olde Great Key Hunt in the morning.*

Oh, she is very pithy in her pith helmet.

But she has a point. I lose my keys on a daily basis, so I drop them into the dish on the coffee table, the crash of keys against glass a cartoon cymbal. I flop down on the couch and stare at the red living room walls, which my mother and I painted and texturized last summer. We had aimed for a field-of-poppies vibe, crisp and vibrant, fluted at the edges, but we ended up with muddy gazpacho. I think of my mom laughing at our failed efforts, of her in her rocker-chick black T-shirt and cutoffs, of how she told me, "This whole Home Depot culture we're living in is bullshit. Pottery Barn can suck it too."

I watch TV for hours, until there are only infomercials for Proactiv and the Ab Roller, until my eyes feel like dried-out moon marbles, but I do not fall asleep like a badass, splayed out on the couch with my gun clutched to my sternum. I lie down in my mother's room, in her queen-sized bed. I should not sleep in her bed; I should not clutter her smell with mine. I want the lemongrass essence and Parliament cigarettes to forever linger on her crumpled sheets. I do not want to kill my mother off with my perfume and hair products and powder-scented deodorant, but we're fading into each other just the same.

But I have something. I have a strange new freedom of heart, which is the gun on my mother's rosewood nightstand. I try to fall into sleep but remain in a state of dreamy wakefulness; I float around Woodrow Wilson High School. I hover close to the water-stained ceiling of the gymnasium, where a pep rally is in full effect: the marching band plays, the glint of brass from tuba and French horn nearly blinds me; the cheerleaders cheer. English teacher Lisa Kaplansky has changed out of her hip linens and clogs into a cheerleading skirt. She has joined all the Megans and Caitlins in yelling *Go, Sandinista! Take it to the hoop!* The teachers and counselors sit in the bleachers with the students, shepherds to the flock. They pelt me with sugarless gum, with Gummi bears.

Catherine Bennett sits in the last row, but of course now she's not so scary; she clutches the teacher's edition of *Math Without Fear!* to her chest and smiles vaguely toward the heavens, toward me, her face a tableau of innocence and early Alzheimer's. She cannot place the floating girl on the ceiling. *Who is that? I really should pay closer attention.* Her eyebrows rise when she notices my creamy pink gun. It has caught her attention.

Alecia Hardaway appears at the doors of the gymnasium,

waving one hand frantically, visoring the other over her forehead as she frowns, puzzled by my gymnasium ascension. *Sandinista? Hi, Sandinista! You're a real cool person every day, Sandinista!*

I hide my gun behind my back as I wave at Alecia Hardaway.

But Catherine Bennett sees my gun—oh, she knows all about my handgun. And so she merely lowers her eyes and clasps her hands, as if she were shy, or kind, or in prayer. But, Mrs. Bennett, switching to sweetheart mode will not impress me now. And it's Mrs. Bennett's getting away with it that gives me the courage to get out of bed and leave the house at four in the morning, though there's nobody waiting for my safe return. But I will have my gun. For now I stick it in the glove box with the box of bullets and so hi ho, hi ho, it's off to the wicked witch's house I go!

Oh, how I love the *ccccahlunk* sound it makes when I turn a corner sharply—the gun escaping the soft, folded maps and candy wrappers and napkins. And I drive, the music cranked, my driving on the slick streets fast enough that it feels like I might ascend and go flying over the guardrails of the interstate to live forever in the iced velvet night. I must be going forty miles over the speed limit, taunting the black ice, but there are no cops around. This is a shame since flashing lights and a soft siren sign would be relief, medicine for this strung-out psycho feeling. And yet my sadness has a metallic edge. I have a gun.

I park across the street from Catherine Bennett's house; I park so I can see the window where I hurled a stone amphibian—such is my courage! Oh, a valorous girl am I! Of course I want to return to the scene of the throwaway crime, to see the thrill of silver duct tape covering up the pane, the fast footprints in the snow. But the side yard of her house is too dark, no light through yonder window breaks for Catherine Bennett, for me. Not even a porch light left on. Her house would disappear in the darkness if not for the snow frosting it like a gingerbread house, a Hansel-and-Gretel getaway for Catherine Bennett. The car is cold. I double check that the doors are locked, thinking that if I were killed outside Catherine Bennett's house when I myself am in possession of a gun, well . . . that would be just my luck indeed. I take my gun out of the glove box and put it on my lap, my little heavy metal baby.

I wonder how it would feel to crunch through the snow yet again, gun in my hand, to walk up to her door and *ding-dong* and *Nice to see you. Might I borrow a cup of sugar?*

My mind floats back to the day last fall when Mrs. Bennett, open algebra book in her hands, started a vicious, free-flowing conversation with Alecia. Mrs. Bennett was plagued by a froggy throat, and so there was a lozenge clacking against her teeth when she announced, apropos of nothing, that she was really looking forward to her Thermos of home-made beef stew. She turned to Alecia and said, as if pleasantly, "By the way, Alecia, what is the meal that a person eats in the middle of the day?"

Here Alecia Hardaway paused, and you could see her processing . . . *Middle of the day . . . middle of the day . . . middle of the day . . .* not quite able to put it together. When she finally answered, it was without her usual *Jeopardy!* player exuberance. Her tentativeness was even more dreadful than the shouted exultations of a slow girl, for it showed that there was something beyond Alecia's grinning outbursts and her glittery Hello Kitty notebooks, that maybe there had always been more to Alecia Hardaway than we had thought.

And so Alecia Hardaway, who was definitely paying attention—her face screwed up and her eyes rolled back, ticking an unknown quantity off on her fingers—hours? heartbreaks?—finally said, "Breakfast?"

And of course the class sighed, and Mrs. Bennett's mouth formed an oval of delight as her eyebrow shot up, the incarnation of her cartoonish evil. "Breakfast, Alecia? Is it really breakfast?"

But it was a trick question; the middle of the day is a variable, depending on the day: on a school day it's high noon, but on the weekend you might sleep late, maybe till noon, which would make breakfast the middle of the day.

And, really, who's the genius now, who doesn't know that I sit outside her house waiting for her with my fake, filmy shroud of innocence? I raise my gun to the cold car window, metal to safety glass. I squeeze one eye shut and aim the barrel at Catherine Bennett's front door. *A boy sets out like something thrown from the furnace of a star.*

Guess what? So does a girl.

But also I know—like the sickly sweet refrain from one of my mother's old Abba albums—*I know, I know, I know, I know,* with God as my witness I know—that Catherine Bennett is beyond all accountability, a true believer in the world of *What? Oh, no! There must have been a misunderstanding. I was just kidding around! Just fooling around! That's my style.* I see that gunning for those she perceives as weak or different is simply part of her DNA. And the school will probably do nothing; maybe they will give Catherine Bennett an expedient pep talk before they aggressively pretend that it never happened. Before they offer me a passive-aggressive apology—*I'm sorry you feel that way*—before they give me a corporate smile and many suggestions. There is a virtual high school in the district; I imagine they might like for me to continue my education online.

Yet how am I any different from all the grinning jackasses of the world? How valiant was I on those days when Catherine Bennett would torment and taunt Alecia Hardaway for sport? Didn't I poison the cake with my own silence? Golly, why did my heart suddenly swell with this intense feeling for the slow girl? Do I really have to be the sort of person who only feels empathy and regret for a persecuted girl once I join her ranks? Do I really have to be so fucking typical? My poor mother, who always championed the underdog, would expect a little better from me.

I lower my gun to my lap. I review some basic facts, hoping for clarity. Right now Catherine Bennett is inside her house and I am outside her house, parked beneath the shaggy evergreen that borders her front lawn. We are both alone in the world—her husband is dead, and . . . I force myself to form the sentence in my head; I spell it out in the choppy font of cartoon ransom notes: my mother is dead. I turn my car on for the heater; I overheat and turn it off, sitting in the cold. I cross my arms over my chest. My rib still hurts, but *I am paying attention.*

I do not listen to the radio or to a CD. I sit in silence—trying to hear what, if anything, God tells me in the heart of this cold Midwestern night, in this reflective blackness that shades the snow in the distance with lilac and navy. I'm thinking, *Out of the depths I cry unto you, O Lord,* and also *I could do it I could do it I could do it.*

FrIDaY
PLaYInG WITH THe cHeeTaHS

I'm wearing starlet shoes and drinking coffee as I hobble from my parked car to the Pale Circus, a short icy journey that, to an indoors-loving girl like me, is as treacherous as a Himalayan trek on stilts. And so I nearly wipe out in my vintage stilettos when I hit a slick patch. I'm correcting myself, arms arched like I'm surfing, when I notice that the headless mannequin is wearing a long white parka with a full and fluffy hood. Our Lady of the Snows. When I pull open the door of the Pale Circus, I find Henry Charbonneau seated at the cash desk. Despite his general quality of bedazzlement— the sweet celery eyes, the ironic look of heartbreak on a face far, far too pretty for anyone to refuse, his startling hands, the knuckles wide as soup spoons—Henry Charbonneau certainly disappoints me. Wherefore art thou, Bradley?

"Good morning, pretty girl, good morning," Henry Charbonneau calls out, as if he were a pet-store parrot with green and blue plumage. "We've got to get you some keys. Your own set, dearie-doo."

"Okay," I say. I will certainly kick off my stilettos later, but for now I hammer across the wooden floor in my lovely and perilous beaded shoes. With each wooden *whackuh whackuh* Henry Charbonneau winces, his central nervous system unglued by my shoes. Oh, he does so love the varnished hardwood of the Pale Circus. . . .

"Bradley called me this morning at home, and, apparently, he wasn't 'feeling well,' " Henry says, hooking his fingers around those two words and giving an exasperated smile, as if we were comrades in the know and Bradley existed merely as a drunken oaf we tolerated out of sheer goodwill.

But I offer up only a concerned and quizzical Florence Nightingale expression, as if Bradley has a new and surprising diagnosis and I am pondering potential sympathies: A balloon bouquet? Banana cream pie?

"I hope he feels better soon."

"Oh, I'm fairly sure it's nothing serious and that he'll be 'feeling better soon,' " Henry Charbonneau says, finger-quoting yet again. "Just as soon as he's had a few hours to sleep off his hangover."

And thinking, *Wow, overkill, dude, what with all the bitchy finger quoting,* I take off my coat and set my coffee cup on the counter.

Though it has a lid, Henry looks at my coffee cup with alarm, as if I'm about to dump it all over the party dresses slung next to the cash register, or maybe slam dance over and splash my coffee on the white fur parka in the display window, an homage to PETA, as the fur is really just acrylic fluff.

I take another sip of my coffee and he rubs his hands together, itching to give me instruction. Like all bosses, Henry Charbonneau believes the wheels of industry should be in motion at all times, that workers should be *working, people, working!* I realize that he's just a hipper and certainly more handsome version of bald Herb Winters, the manager at Baskin-Robbins, who gave many tutorials in the wrist-flip that provided maximum speed and efficiency when I was scooping up the Mint Chip and Pralines 'n Cream last summer.

Henry Charbonneau smiles at me, rests his palm on the party dresses before he taps them and says, "Will you iron these up, love?"

Ironing is not in my skill set. My mother was a leather-jacket-and-jeans kind of gal; in summer, a lover of Indian cotton gauze glinting with metallic thread. I take my vintage clothes to the dry cleaner's. There is no iron in my home. And when I'm at the Pale Circus I prefer to use the steam cleaner with its fat-frog mouth sagging away from the hose that connects it to the steam.

But what can I do when he's already plugging in the iron

and pushing the candy and cash register aside, covering the cash desk with a stained tea towel. Oh, *that's* what they're for. I used the towel to mop up spilled tea yesterday. Henry Charbonneau notices the sepia-colored stains. Tut-tutting a bit, he digs around under the counter, finds a clean tea towel and drapes it over the cash desk.

I take another sip of coffee, and Henry Charbonneau says, "This time, before there are many customers, is really a *great* time to do all the housekeeping."

"Right," I say brightly, thinking *Jackass,* and I take a long draw of coffee before I flip my cup into the painted lavender trash can.

I lay a magenta dress with a jewel collar on the counter and start nosing the warm iron down the pleat of the skirt. I make a smooth canal; I am paying attention. I follow the line of the pleats and am rewarded by a dramatic smoothness, one crisp, bright line shooting to the hem.

I am lost in the reverie of this magic when Catherine Bennett's gray face pops into my mind, entirely un-fucking-bidden: there she is, there she is, as if she doesn't know I have a pink and cream gun in my glove box. This morning I left it on the coffee table, and then reconsidered. And so I'm thinking of the gun and bullets in my glove box when the iron grazes my pinkie. I pop my finger into my mouth, and Henry Charbonneau looks over, alarmed, as if this action is totally unhygienic/porn star–ish. Which, I suppose, it is.

"You okay?" he asks.

"I'm fine," I say in a singsong voice.

Henry straightens a few racks, gives a brisk *tsk tsk!* to a cashmere cardigan with a rip at the elbow before he checks the price tag, and seems to consider it for a moment. Henry Charbonneau sighs and then brightens, perhaps assigning a certain vagabond charm to the sweater, and rehangs it.

I finish ironing the first dress, hang it on a satin-covered hanger, and start on a spring-green shantung shift. The fabric sizzles and I turn down the temperature wheel. I find a soothing rhythm to my ironing; I lose myself in the steam and heated fabrics, and I think of my gun in my glove box, and it does make me feel better; it seems to cancel out the power of the unringing cell phone in my pocket, the cheap little Sprint freebie that has made me hope's bitch. I try to discipline myself—I will check my home messages on my lunch hour and not a minute before.

The bells on the door shiver and then ring out and it's Erika in a scarlet-red coat, ripped fishnets and combat boots, her dark, manicured nails popping out of her fingerless gloves like chocolates. She's holding a bakery box. "Henry, you old slag. Sandinista's ironing and you're just mincing about?"

"What is it *this* time?" Henry asks, as if morose.

Erika opens the bakery box like a game-show hostess and caresses the air over the candy. "Today we have chocolate caramels infused with fresh pineapple juice."

Erika holds out the box, and Henry says, "Oh, that sounds like it will be good for a gentleman's waistline."

But he takes one anyway. He chews, rolling his eyes and holding up one finger, imploring us to *wait, wait!* And then, the verdict: "That is, in all seriousness, the best thing I've ever had in my mouth."

Erika smiles at me and stage-whispers: "We will be

ladies, and let the obvious punch line to that joke just fade, fade, fade away." She twinkles her fingers back and forth, Glinda the Good Witch, bidding sweet farewell to the bawdy, the improper, and hands me the box of chocolates.

"Later, babies," she says. "I'm off to the sugar mines."

We watch Erika cross the street, the tails of her red coat whipping behind her.

"She's a genius with the chocolates, Sandinista. She used to be the pastry chef at Boulangerie Marcel."

Henry Charbonneau has the look of someone wanting very badly to tell you something that you do not particularly want to hear. I place Erika's chocolates in the mahogany display box.

"She was raped at gunpoint going into the bakery one morning before dawn. Someone knew the pastry chef went in at four-thirty. Someone was waiting for Erika."

Henry Charbonneau's gaze turns from the anticipatory to the rueful, as if saying it out loud has cost him something. He looks down at the floors of the Pale Circus for a moment. But soon he's distracted by a scuff, a nick, something. He leans down and works his fingers over the wood with a stern *tsk*.

"She opened her own bakery after it happened. Everyone was pretty surprised that she went the way of pornography. But"—he waves his hand in the air, *c'est la vie*—"it's quite common for victims to take on the ways of their oppressors."

I think of the frosting in the bowl. This professor of gently used couture might not be quite as clever as he thinks.

"Stockholm syndrome," he muses dreamily, stretching the words into a musical affliction that sounds like it would strike down blond supermodels. "I do believe she has Stockholm syndrome."

"Oh?"

"Well, it's back to work for us!" He claps his hands, and I get the message—how could I not—and finish ironing a black polished cotton shirt with a severe bell shape. When I look up, I find Henry Charbonneau slacking, gazing out the window, watching the monks troop past in their brown robes—which, I guess, preclude their need for winter coats.

Henry Charbonneau turns from the window and looks at me; he's clutching a bottle of Windex to his chest like a bouquet of bluebells, like he's a tidy bridesmaid. "Do you like working here?"

"I love it," I say, truthfully.

Henry Charbonneau nods. "I *knew* you would," he says. When he looks down at the floor with a shy smile I see what it is about him that causes Bradley's face to be wreathed in kittenish pain—oh, the sexy, intermittent kindness of Henry Charbonneau. Except soon he completely dispenses with his facade of cleaning and sits down, yoga-style, near the front window, with a book.

I am nearly undone by his feudal tendencies, as I still have a mound of satin dresses to iron. But the ironing is a small, good thing, even if my pleats totally suck. I have seen Bradley do twenty pleats in the time it takes me to iron three, and his pleats are severe and fresh.

When Henry looks at all these dresses I have ironed, he

will sigh and his face will crumple. But for now I work and my mind wanders to my first short film of the day, which showcases my own Great Expectations:

We first meet Lisa Kaplansky when she is in the classroom, a hip teacher sitting cross-legged on her desk, comfy in her Dansko clogs, black yoga pants and batik tunic. Ms. Kaplansky is being apprised of the school situation by the several caring students crowded around her desk, Bethany Adams chief among them. Bethany Adams, Sandinista Jones's best friend from elementary school. In junior high Sandinista dumped Bethany for a skag named Josie Jennings, a bad call, the outlaw cadence of Josie's name a glimpse into her very soul. But Bethany Adams is as tall as a catalog model and a star volleyball player, to boot; she has fared well, even with those junior high injustices. And now Bethany Adams spills it with feeling. "And remember, Ms. Ka-plansky, Sandinista's mother died in the fall." Here I rework the sentence, I slide the words back into Bethany's mouth so that it doesn't sound like my mother stepped off a sky-scraper: *"And remember, Ms. Kaplansky, Sandinista's mother died last autumn. She's all alone in the world this year."*

Lisa Kaplansky's face falls and goes gray and red all at once, a crumbling ash rose. She says: "Class, I'll be back." Her tunic billows out behind her as she scrambles off the desk and flies out of the room. Lisa Kaplansky charges into the principal's office without knocking, only to find a man who is neither prince nor pal, an antihero, perhaps the Antichrist: Principal Jack Johnson. He is cruising the Net for "artistic photos" and he hammers the escape button with his index finger when he sees Lisa Kaplansky.

"Catherine Bennett . . . ," Ms. Kaplansky says, breathless.

"I know," he says. He lets loose with a desolate little sigh. "I've heard all about it by now."

Because his demeanor veers too close to the ol' "hey, babe, these things happen" nonchalance of the professional educator, Lisa Kaplansky plants a hand on Jack Johnson's desk. Because she hits the tanning beds—I fear you not, melanoma!—her hand is a plasticine shade of butterscotch, and she wears a silver skull ring on her middle finger with ominous violet stones in the carved eye sockets, Georgia O'Keeffe for the aging hipster. Still, despite a few fashion missteps, Lisa Kaplansky is valiant, pure-hearted.

"Catherine Bennett?" Lisa Kaplansky rolls the words off her tongue—the last name clipped and ominous, like a dare. "She kicked Sandinista's desk!"

They lock eyes.

"I dunno," he says. "She's been here forever. It's complicated."

"You have two choices," Lisa Kaplansky says. "Fire her today or I go to the newspaper tomorrow."

Eager to get back to his photographs, Jack Johnson nods. Fantasy sequence number two:

Wherein we find the class sitting quietly after Mrs. Bennett and Sandinista exit, ye olde calm after the storm: there sits Evan Harper in his CORPORATE COFFEE SUCKS T-shirt, inscrutable as you please. Alecia Hardaway reads her Powerpuff Girls comic book, her face seized by some secret delight, or maybe it's merely the madcap antics of crime-fighting cupcakes. A few girls are sniffling. A few boys are thinking poetic and unsavory thoughts of Sandinsta Jones, wondering, Why are the beautiful ones always so tormented?

Mr. Hale, the gym teacher, is back from escorting Mrs. Bennett to the office. He has told everyone, "Why don't we just have some quiet time before the bell rings." And so he sits at Mrs. Bennett's desk, reading Penthouse, which he has stashed between the covers of an ancient Newsweek. And all is quiet; all is still. But, people, all is not calm, nor is it bright.

Sandinista Jones is walking back into the school. Sandinista must have done some kind of Superman outfit switcheroo in her car, because she's returning to Woodrow Wilson High School in a wrap dress with repeating black and turquoise triangles and patent-leather high heels. In her matching patent-leather handbag there is a gun. Sandinista Jones walks through the dim anteroom of the principal's office unobserved, the secretary listening to her iPod and reading T. S. Eliot. Sandinista Jones looks through the rectangular windowpane of the principal's office and sees Catherine Bennett holding up a platter covered with Saran Wrap. Sandinista Jones puts her head next to the cracked door, and Sandinista Jones pays attention.

"Caramel apples?" Catherine Bennett smiles and flutters her pale lashes. She is one grotesque coquette.

"What?" asks Principal Jack Johnson. He looks frightened.

"You know I bring them to the Christmas party every year!"

Catherine Bennett plunks the platter down on his desk and frantically takes off the Saran Wrap. "It's kind of my signature treat! I bring them to class sometimes and let the kids graze a bit while they do their math problems. Did you know if they get an A on their test I also give them a coupon for a free burrito?"

Through the cold patent leather of her handbag, Sandinista Jones feels the bulk of her gun.

The principal clears his throat. "I was wondering if we might talk a little bit about Sandinista Jones? The . . . incident."

"Nice, girl, nice girl! What a super senior class we have!" Catherine Bennett pushes the platter of apples closer to Jack Johnson. "You have to use Red Delicious. They have to be very, very firm! Or else the warm caramel will turn the apples to pure goosh." She gives a Halloween grimace and repeats "pure goosh" in a Frankenstein monotone. She flutters her hands to her neck and leaves them there. She laughs and says lightly, "Pure goosh," and looks out the window at the lemon-gray sky of a dreary afternoon, the banked snow. She whispers, "Pure goosh."

The gun in Sandinsta's purse is an itch, an ache.

But, now, in Jack Johnson, Sandinista Jones sees something beyond the random expedient pervy principal; she sees a certain wariness, the briefest sign of cognition. Jack Johnson looks down at the caramel apples, all that red and tan sweetness on his desk, fructose and sucrose and corn syrup goosing his brains by osmosis: Oh, fuck. Catherine Bennett really is crazy.

And this is all Sandinista Jones wants, this gift of someone who gets it, who is not going to fake-smile and give her zombie eyes: Have you perhaps misinterpreted the situation? And Jack Johnson is getting it slowly, surely. . . . He rubs his temple and thinks of Catherine Bennett's erratic behavior in the teachers' lounge; he thinks of a random Monday morning before school started when he heard a pounding in the hall and looked out to see Catherine Bennett banging her fist against every locker, remembers how the sound reverberated down the hall like a metallic woodpecker. . . .

Sandinista Jones opens the door to the principal's office.

Catherine Bennett says, "Well, look who's here! Speak of the devil! Hi, Sandinista!"

Sandinista Jones looks at Jack Johnson and says, "Through your faith, you have earned your salvation. Go in peace."

And he does, the principal grabs his coffee cup from his desk and skitters out of his office. Next, Sandinista turns to Mrs. Bennett, who sits with her hands clasped together, smiling.

The interlocking silver circle on Sandinista Jones's leather handbag makes an intriguing swarishhh when she clicks it open.

But then the string of bells on the door shivers and Bradley walks into the Pale Circus and smiles at me, big and sweet; he gives a repentant nod to Henry Charbonneau, who offers up a tart. "So nice of you to join us, Bradley."

The sight of Bradley gives me a jolt of optimism that makes me start to think a little differently. Because maybe Catherine Bennett's car parked in the lot could mean many things: she could have already been dismissed from her teaching job, and in a flurry of whacked-out desperation, maybe she really has brought a tray of candied fruit to the principal and staff; perhaps she has already morphed into the crazy aunt at the Christmas party. Surely they are trying to find a way to let her go quietly. Lisa Kaplansky could be waiting to call and tell me about the terms of Catherine Bennett's dismissal. The words *terms of dismissal* are bright and promising as poppies, and when Ms. Kaplansky tells me about Catherine Bennett's terms of dismissal, orange-red blossoms will flower through my mind. I will nod and look pensively to the ceiling, an intelligent girl considering a fact.

Oh, I will not disappoint Lisa Kaplansky. I will not scream or shout about the injustice shown to me, I will simply say, *I see,* and I will be appreciative of the school's efforts as I gnaw my thumbnail, taking it all in, and who among you would not admire my stoicism, who among you would not note the jaunty poppy-colored cashmere-sweater-and-beret combo I am wearing in this five-second daydream?

At the very least, I imagine that everyone has told their parents and that the parents have probably called the school and it is all a bit of a breathless mess. I also understand that people clear up business on Friday afternoons; there is an implicit decency to clearing up any old business so that people might be free to enjoy their weekends—viva Miller time!—the same week as *the incident* . . . because there is a certain decency to taking care of things within the week. It's professional. And so the chance of me getting the call today is high . . . at least, moderately high. . . .

Bradley looks at the pile of dresses still to be ironed and then back at Henry Charbonneau, who is reading in the pale morning sun. To anyone passing on the street this must make a fetching picture, the headless mannequin in her polar parka and Henry Charbonneau with his book and fashionably pensive gaze: a portrait of the artist as a not-so-young man.

Bradley swallows his laughter, but his shoulders shake a little bit as he takes off his leather jacket. Bradley whispers: "It is *such* a shame that Henry Charbonneau was born after the Civil War. Because just look at the dear man. He would have looked fetching drinking mint juleps and reading on some crumbling, leafy veranda while his slaves hammered horseshoes and hung out laundry under the blazing sun."

Henry doesn't look up from his book when he says, "Bradley, if you're both half an hour late to work and mocking me . . . hmm . . . that doesn't necessarily seem like a wise combination."

Bradley smiles. "Observation is not mockery."

"Listen up, worker bees." Henry Charbonneau clears his throat. "I'm going to read a poem."

I look down and take a ferocious interest in a satin mandarin collar, tracing the mouth of the iron around the sweet curves. Because the only thing more mortifying than someone reading a poem out loud is having someone read their *own* poetry out loud, but as Henry is reading from a book and not a frayed spiral notebook, at least I won't be party to that cringe-fest. And so the sun sparkles and Bradley gives me a comradely smile and Henry Charbonneau begins his recitation:

> *"The monastery is quiet. Seconal*
> *drifts down upon it from the moon.*
> *I can see the lights*
> *of the city I came from,*
> *can remember how a boy sets out*
> *like something thrown from the furnace*
> *of a star. In the conflagration of memory*
> *my people sit on green benches in the park,*
> *terrified, evil, broken by love—*
> *to sit with them inside that invisible fire*
> *of hours day after day while the shadow of the milk*

> billboard crawled across the street
> seemed impossible, but how
> was it different from here,
> where they have one day they play over
> and over as if they think
> it is our favorite, and we stay
> for our natural lives,
> a phrase that conjures up the sun's
> dark ash adrift after ten billion years
> of unconsolable burning?"

"Look," Bradley says.

Right on cue, two of our monks, the monks of St. Joseph's, walk past. Caught in the bright spell, the three of us look out at them with longing. When they pass out of view, Henry Charbonneau says: "It's a Denis Johnson poem. My book club is reading his poetry this week. But, truthfully, I think I might be the only one to 'get it,'" he says, making air quotes around the last two words.

My heart races a bit. "So is Arne in your book club?"

Henry Charbonneau looks truly surprised. "Have you been hanging out at the pawnshop, Sandinista? And yes, Arne is most certainly in my book club. And, well, how have you become a girl from around the way so quickly?"

Bradley smiles at me and I can *feel* it, the bright promise of the New Testament, my phone ringing at home, as if Jesus himself is calling, using his human's voice, which is the commingling of Joe Strummer's and Al Green's and Bono's, saying, *I will not leave you comfortless, I will come to you.*

We get into the groove of the day: Henry Charbonneau

leaves to do the important things that Henry Charbonneau must do and Bradley and I iron dresses and fill candy dishes; we offer up kindness to strangers who walk into the Pale Circus—though, no, this does not include letting them use the bathroom—we arrange and rearrange clothes; we mourn the implicit broken contract and personal disappointment of gorgeous clothes balled up on the dressing room floor, left there by some jackass customers. We rehang these spurned items, cursing.

I hope that my mother can see the good moments of this day, my camaraderie with Bradley; I hope my mother can see me working alongside a boy who keeps Catherine Bennett at bay with fun and fabrics.

I hope my mother can see me laughing at a boy's joke: Bradley, apropos of nothing, sniffs the air with great distaste. He says, "Uggh. It smells like up-dog in here."

I look up from the last unironed dress in my stack and say: "*What* is up-dog?"

"Not much, dog. Wazzup with you?"

And then we laugh the high, keening laughter that reminds me of our old neighbor's hunting dog, the intergalactic noises he would make as the elderly Mr. Schmitz packed up his truck for a day of hunting. A skinny, liver-spotted dog who lived for the crack of the gun.

* * *

Bradley seems unwilling to risk taking a lunch hour thirty minutes after he shows up for work, so I cruise down Thirty-Eighth Street by myself.

My car knows where to go. It's as if the Taurus is some futuristic Ford that can read my mind and poof, purple haze, the rabbit out of the hat, three dollars in gas, I'm turning in to the parking lot. With my gun in my glove box I'm as amped as a prizefighter. I'm at Woodrow Wilson High School at 12:30 smack on the nose, on the cauliflower ears.

I park way in the back row, where the newspaper recycling vat intersects the mouth of the track, and watch my fellow seniors with off-campus lunch privileges come out of school: even from this distance I can spot a few stoner pals, and there is the surly cheerleader, Olivia Leland, who I was friends with until seventh grade, until her mother learned that my house was slightly too crappy and also in the wrong part of town. But fair enough, there is also Johanna Zehr, whom I promptly dumped when I started high school, as she had committed the double sin of not smoking Camel Lights and enjoying Christian rock. Until freshman year I loved Johanna both for her Mennonite beauty—blond cornsilk hair pulled into a bridal bun at the crown of her head—and for the luscious cinnamon buns her mother baked. Even in my current gloom I think of her mother's being so pleased that I could eat three, how she wrote out the directions for me on an index card—*Use water from boiled potatoes.*

Why did the potato water make the cinnamon buns so delicious?

My car fills with the smell of cinnamon and warm frosting as the senior cliques trickle out of school, as the security guard roams the parking lot with his hand clapped to the walkie-talkie clipped to his belt, wishing it were a billy club or better yet, a gun, probably wishing he were an actual police officer, which would make it ever so easy for him to get laid. Instead he's stuck being a minimum-wager for the school security corporation that blossomed after the shootings at Columbine.

I light a cigarette and watch the teachers who smoke heading out to their cars for a quickie, and then there she is, her herky-jerky walk, her crazy-ass smile: Catherine Bennett. She wheels a backpack behind her, as if harboring a long-lost dream of being a flight attendant. She is going to lunch, I suppose. She either has a cell phone clipped to her ear or is frantically talking to herself. Her hair is short. I don't see a phone. See how she walks with purpose—*Look alive, people! Pay attention! Alecia, Sandinista, are you paying attention? Have you done the review problems? Why are you wearing a sweater? Did someone not check the weather forecast?* Oh, she is the Comet in my cake and will be forfuckingever if I don't do something.

But I think of the boys at Columbine, how stupid and wild-hearted they were with their boy-dreams of shooting everybody up. And not just the teachers and the kids who had bullied them, but random people, nice people: the Johanna Zehrs of the world, some of them dead, some of them forever tethered to wheelchairs and catheters, thanks to the faulty, self-aggrandizing logic of tortured dorks. Henry Charbonneau's poetry recital floats back to me as I replay the old news footage from Columbine in my head: *a boy sets out like something thrown from the furnace of a star.* Stupid, stupid, stupid.

And Erika's poisoned porno cake is not the best idea

either. Has she not thought it out? Because it's so easy to imagine the stripper leaving the drunken guys in the living room—*See ya, boys!*—and heading out to the kitchen, to the safety of her coat and boots stashed by the fridge. She steals a beer for herself, for later when she is relaxing in the tub, and cuts a piece of cake up for her daughter. She takes the green frosted section, the bikini underpants, thinking how it is the exact shade of Mr. Ribbits, her daughter's stuffed frog.

Precision. Accuracy. It's best to work with a clear plan.

Mrs. Bennett stows her little suitcase in her trunk and gets into her car. It seems that the clouds have parted just for her, that a single brush of sunlight illuminates her Toyota Corolla, her bumper sticker a warning to all: WELL-BEHAVED WOMEN RARELY MAKE HISTORY!

But then the thoughts I have actively been pushing from my brain rush back to me. Mrs. O'Dell, the biology teacher, coming in the day when she heard Catherine Bennett using her "funny" tone with Alecia and yelling at her for forgetting her backpack. "And you have no idea where you put it? Is that it? I'm just supposed to let you wander the halls alone?" How Mrs. O'Dell looked down over her half-glasses as she entered the classroom, as if delivering an important paper, walking purposefully to Catherine Bennett's desk. How Mrs. Bennett looked up and said "Oh! Good morning, Jean!" when she saw Mrs. O'Dell. How she then smiled, rolled her eyes at Alecia as if they were actresses in a 1940s student-teacher screwball comedy. When I walked past Mrs. Bennett's desk on the way out of class, I looked at the piece of paper: blank.

And worse, the day Ms. Kaplansky saw Mrs. Bennett walking down the hall, Mrs. Bennett pounding her fist to the palm of her hand, the odd, skin-slap sound of it as she muttered under her breath. We had studied "The Dead" in Lisa Kaplansky's class that morning, a chilly golden-green September morning. When Mrs. Bennett passed Lisa Kaplansky—*slap! slap!*—Lisa Kaplansky allowed a frown to grip the space between her eyebrows, the briefest parenthesis, before Lisa Kaplansky looked away and smiled brightly as if she had just seen something very pleasing indeed: all that snow covering the living and the dead.

* * *

After lunch, the day goes gray and teary: a bitchy customer inquiring about the discount for a tear in the lining of wool tuxedo pants sends me catapulting into a fit of OCD message-checking, my overused cell phone hot as a soup pan against my ear. Because this is it. Friday afternoon. The school's last chance to make this right before the weekend, before Monday's events go all into the muzzy whirl of *Okay. Now, when did this happen?* This is it, my last best chance for Lisa Kaplansky or the principal or anyone to call.

I am one with Bradley because he does this too; he's Mr. Ringy to my Ms. Dingy with his constant cell-phone checking. He is straightening a rack of shoes, all the pointy toes as tense as good girls lined up in pairs at a dance. His phone is cradled between his shoulder and his ear.

But Bradley has received good news.

I see it in his smile, in his exhilarated Swiffering, in the way he tosses me a velvet cape and says, "Buy this! You'll be more beautiful than Batgirl, Sandinista!" And goddamn, still no messages for me—not even one reminder call for a dentist appointment. It's as if the whole world is colluding with the school to accentuate the truth: nobody's paying attention.

* * *

When we lock up the Pale Circus, Bradley leaves in a flurry; he gives me one last "You okay? Your car's right across the street, right? I'll see you tomorrow, okay?" And off he goes down the sidewalk with his jacket slung over his shoulder, with his palpable delight. With, really, no thought of me.

I walk across the snowy street and lean on my car.

I try one last time: I dial my cell phone, hoping that there is magic in the lavender twilight, and I try to believe that the world is full of promise and stricken beauty but . . . *beep! You have no new messages.*

So, to be sure, one thing the world is not full of is concerned people picking up the phone to check on your welfare. The cell phone is cold against my ear, but I hold it there anyway, and I think of the child who licked the street pole and got his tongue stuck. Perhaps I will freeze the phone to my ear in homage to Catherine Bennett and getting away with it, in homage to me and to Alecia Hardaway, to all the other screwed daughters of Eve who have walked through her classroom. I am contemplating how deeply symbolic the phone earring would make me look—*I am waiting for the world to call*—but then there's also the possibility of looking like any random sweatpanted jackass who wears a Bluetooth clamped to his or her ear, as if expecting communication from Mars, when I see the monk.

He's walking down the street, hands clasped behind his back. Why are the wandering Jesus people so lame? Why do they do nothing but smile and stroll around in their soft sandals in the snow and cold? Okay, I suppose that inside the monastery they are praying in their cells, maybe stretching their arms out and tilting their heads to the left, making Bambi eyes and lolling their mouths open in extracurricular imitation of the cruciform Jesus in his hour of betrayal. And I suppose some monks are working at the monastery, creating jams and jellies, an image that brings to mind 1940s farmwives in gingham aprons and strawberries on the vine, a summer day on the banks of the Kaw, though probably the real work is strictly industrial: boiling and dangerous.

I put my cell phone in my pocket and walk toward the monk. I have a bounce in my step, a purposefulness born of absolutely nothing. The monk smiles at me. He's wearing a wool beret, which gives him the look of a French film director. The beret makes me think of the Madeline stories my mother read to me when I was a child: "'In an old house in Paris that was covered with vines' . . . I can't wait to take you to Paris someday, Sandinista!" Of course the City of Light was on the itinerary for our postgraduation trip. But now it's just me; it's just me and a random monk whose eyebrows shoot up as he realizes that I am walking away from my car, not haphazardly window-shopping at the liquor store, but coming straight to him. But Jesus boy should not be so worried, for I am giving him a polite smile, striding along happily like the wholesome Midwestern girl that I am not. I am Midwestern to the extreme, which my mother guarded against: "You don't have to be nice to everyone all the time, at all times." But as the smiling monk comes closer he infuriates me. His big, nervous smile makes me want to chew off my arm, and the whole sandals-in-the-snow thing is a bit ostentatious, a bit too *And Jesus Loves Thy Frozen Toes*–ish.

"Well, good evening," the monk says, hearty and polite as Santa—he even has a huge bushy beard.

"Well, hello!" I double his exuberance. I triple it, giving him a brightly psychotic smile and clapping my hands. I have on my mother's shaggy yarn mittens, so my hands make a soft thud instead of a skin slap.

The monk draws his eyebrows together; he puts his hands on his waist and tilts his head back: a rehearsed gesture, I imagine. A pregnant pause. They must teach these conceits in the monastery. But I wait him out. I keep still and smile, a foot soldier of quiet good cheer. I lock eyes with him and struggle not to blink. Finally the monk realizes that if he wants to escape me, he will have to make further social effort.

"I'm Brother Bill," he says.

"I'm Sandinista." I put my hand to my heart, a wintry coquette, and give a little bow. His smile fades as he tries to assess my wacko factor.

Brother Bill asks, "How are you doing today?"

"I'm fine, thanks."

Thank you for asking! I am so great! Great! Oh, my God, I'm just so fabulous. I'm watching my mother and Catherine Bennett and Alecia Hardaway skip around the periphery of the sidewalk, Brother Bill. And, FYI: I believe that all my anger and all my sadness are about to funnel together into a substance that, if measured and bottled, could be sold as a potion that would allow you to body-slam your opponent with one sip. And how are you today, Brother Bill?

Oh, but I don't know why I'm letting this bother me so much; I don't know why I thought the school would call, I don't know why I'm such a sucker, I don't know why I thought my mother would live forever, I don't know why I never said anything when Mrs. Bennett would torment Alecia Hardaway, why I shamefully sat with the rest of the class waiting for the harshly fluorescent-lit moment of Alecia's humiliation to pass.

Brother Bill laces his hands together as if he's about to do that hand game: *Here is the church, here is the steeple, open it up and see all the people.* Instead he nervously pops his knuckles, one by one, each joint offering up a satisfying *crack crack crack.* He is very tall and the clouds are shifting around his head and he looks puzzled and pained, every inch the Christ figure—oh, brother.

"How are *you*?" I ask.

"Oh, fair to midland," he says.

"Well then," I say. "A weather metaphor. Clever."

He puts his hand down at the sides of his robes, palms flat, and seems surprised that he has no pockets, that he is wearing a long robe, and I wonder if he is new to monkdom. He looks about fifty, but maybe he's a slow learner. Like me.

And Alecia. He crosses his arms over his chest. He hunches over a little bit, rubbing his elbows and looking down at the dirty snow. Jesus, he's just out for a walk.

My problems are not his fault and I feel some spark of shame, which may be my mother tapping me with her far-off lightning rod, because, as she liked to say, "Our family value is kindness."

My mother's wisdom, which was often dispensed from fortune-cookie fortunes taped to the refrigerator—*It is no small feat to improve the quality of the day! Lucky numbers 17, 3, 58*—counts for nothing in the real world of screamers and liars. And I see that my moment of bitchiness, my weather-metaphor comment, has made me feel calmer, pensive. If this is a general phenomenon—the bitchier you are, the better you feel!—then after Catherine Bennett's freak-out she must have been the embodiment of post-yoga calm; possibly she was comatose.

"Well, have a great night," I say, mixing it up, trying not to seem too crazy, and failing.

"Thank you," he says. He runs his tongue over his bottom lip, which is lacy with dried skin. *Stop,* I want to say, *that is only going to make it worse.*

When I turn to go he smiles and says, "Hey!"

I smile. I wait. His eyes go blank. Then he focuses and asks, "What animal should you never play cards with?"

"What?" I say, thinking it's a real question, before I see his frantic smile—and then, oh, okay, it's a joke. Sure.

"Well, I don't know," I say, smiling. "What animal should you never play cards with? No idea."

"A cheetah," he says.

I nod. A cheetah.

Is he fucking kidding me? This is his God-given wisdom? Some lame joke from a Dixie Cup?

"Okay," I say, trying to infuse my voice with as much sarcasm as possible. "I will certainly take that under advisement."

"Good," Brother Bill says. He frowns and mumbles under his breath, lots of consonants, lots of *shhh* and *rhhh*. And so now I see—I think I see—that he has something wrong with him. A little something? Like all of us, I guess, but maybe a little more, maybe he was once Alecia Hardaway in the junior high special ed classes, maybe he was once Alecia Hardaway, mainstreamed in algebra class. And so if he wants to spend his adult life making fancy jam and loving Christ and telling kindergarten jokes, well, okay, bring it, Brother Bill. There's no reason I should be such an ass to him.

I try to smile in a normal manner, with no irony or anger, without my gums bared. "Well! Nice talking to you."

"Enjoy your day," he says. I look back at him standing there, pale and nervous in the royal purple twilight. As an afterthought, he offers up a shrill, shouted "Peace be with you!"

I turn away to walk to my cold car, then shout over my shoulder: "You too, Brother Bill."

* * *

The weekend! No plans! It's Miller time, friends, Oh, yes, yes yes yes yes, it is. There's the long, lonesome whistle, where's my local bar? I know there's nobody and nothing for me at home, so I go for a little drive. I feel the need for instruction. And so I find the business card with the gun info and I light out for the territory of Price's Pistol Range.

Price's Pistol Range is just off the interstate and adjacent to a low-rent strip mall—apparently you can learn to blow someone's head off and then walk across the parking lot to World of Nails and get a pedicure for $19.99. When I walk in and see the sign posted at the reception desk—NO MINORS PERMITTED WITHOUT PARENT OR GUARDIAN—I feel a shot to the heart, a metallic pang of *Mom!* But it's not like she would have ever taken me to an indoor shooting range for recreational purposes. The thought *If only my mother were here* seems to belong to the old world now.

The receptionist, a smiling blond woman in her fifties, says: "Can I help you, hon?"

I look up and see myself in the security-TV screen over her head. I shake my hair: the Veronica Lake I created this morning with a Chi iron has frizzed into a Stevie Nicks. Behind the reception desk is a metal door that looks like it might lead to a bank vault.

"Um . . . yes . . . actually . . ." I take the business card that Arne gave me out of my purse and hand it to her, as if this is my entry into a posh private club. Which it might be. "A friend recommended this place to me." I clear my throat. "And, well, I was just looking into taking some classes, or signing up for a lesson, or something."

I'm speaking too fast. I have the adrenaline of a furious, starving jackal.

"Sure, hon. You have your driver's license on you?"

I open my purse and give her my license. She writes the number down on a piece of paper on her clipboard and then looks back up at me and smiles, tapping her baby-pink fingernail on my driver's license. "This is certainly you. But do you have a second form of ID, hon? Anything else with your picture on it?"

I take my school ID from my wallet and hand it to her with a heavy heart.

She looks at my lame school picture for a long, uncomfortable moment. Her creepy smile is so serene it appears as if she's gazing at a photo of an infant in a pastel sweater coat, as if she's about to bust out with a long *awww!* Finally, she looks up and hands me my IDs.

"What an unusual name you have, Sandinista: Sandinista. It's very pretty."

I shrug. "Yeah, it's okay, I guess. . . . Thanks."

She hands me my own clipboard and instructs me to fill out the back and front sides of all the forms. And it becomes increasingly clear that it's hard to go incognito at a shooting range. They want to know who I am and where I live, my social security number, my place of employment and have I ever been convicted of a felony? Have I been convicted of a felony in the past seven years? Of course, I would be a fifth-grade felon had I been convicted of any crime beyond then, but: *Whatever, gun people!*

I sit down in a white wicker chair and notice the cigarette burns in the mauve carpet. At first I'm both confused about the aggressively girly decor and distracted by the magazines on the white coffee table: Along with the usual crumpled copies of *People* and *US Weekly* is a pristine, mailbox-fresh issue of *The New Yorker*. But then I puzzle out that the shooting range has the same vibe as the free dental clinic, which always has the latest issue of *The Economist* in their magazine rack. The management is trying to offer you so much respect regardless of your low income or your questionable desire for a handgun that it comes off a tad patronizing: *We know it's not your fault you don't have dental insurance and thought you might like some pithy social commentary about the free market. We don't think your desire to fire guns for sport makes you a redneck and sincerely hope you enjoy the latest Alice Munro short story.*

I slog through the forms before I pause at my favorite question: *What firearm will you be using today?*

I leave that one blank. I give the forms back to the receptionist with a flurry of nervous lies. I'm so paranoid that she's already made an assessment of my true nature, my true quest, that I try to make it look like I'm a different kind of psycho than I really am.

"So, I just wanted to sign up for some classes, or something. I'm also thinking of taking a martial arts class. I'm really interested in the empowerment of women? I sort of think that gun ownership is a feminist issue." I almost choke on my corn-dog pomposity: certainly Catherine Bennett feels very empowered to treat women in whatever way she pleases. "Primarily I'm interested in self-defense!"

Self-defense. I say it brightly and it has that high and lonesome sound of a mammoth lie: the dog ate my homework!

"Sure," the receptionist says. She picks up the phone and presses a button. "Hey, sweetie, we've got someone out front"—she pauses to smile up at me—"a nice young woman who's interested in a lesson if you've got a few minutes."

I hold up my hand and interrupt her, whispering, "No, no, I didn't mean . . . right now. . . . I meant like, in the future. Maybe next week?"

"Sure, hon." It's unclear whether she's talking to me or the person on the phone. She pumps some lotion out of an economy-sized bottle—Jergens Shea Butter—and smooths it over her hands.

And then there's a buzz, the metal door to the back swings open, and a bony, birdlike woman with a sporty coiffed auburn hairdo emerges, all aflutter, the sleeves of her silk blouse flashing lavender and lime-green ovals and rectangles.

As if seen though a handheld kaleidoscope, the print of her blouse fractures and turns into the paisley print of Catherine Bennett's slip. I close my eyes for a second and then open them again, trying to clear the image from my mind.

"Hello! I'm Shirley, the range master. Tell me what I can help you with. And by the way, you're so pretty. Your hair is darling! Aren't you a doll?" She turns and stage-whispers to the receptionist, "What a living doll!"

I smile, suckered by her compliments. "Thanks. I just wanted to learn a little bit about self-defense. I just thought I would be proactive. There are a lot of burglaries in my neighborhood."

"This is the place! Did you bring your own firearm or do you want to rent one?"

I answer her question with my own: "I'll rent one? I guess?"

"We'll get it done," Shirley says.

And God bless America, I can rent a handgun simply by filling out another form and plunking down my Visa card. In my past life, the one that ended Monday, I could never have imagined a gun-rental charge showing up on my bill. The thought of the stack of unopened mail on the kitchen table gives me a burst of anxiety—last month I forgot to pay the Discover bill, a costly mistake with all the added-on fees. Even with the electric bill and the water bill paid directly out of my mother's savings account—out of my savings account— every month, there's still the problem of making sure I dig my cell-phone bill out of the stack, my home phone bill, the Internet bill. How did my mother find the time to deal with all these shockingly boring details? I have the vague memory of us in line at the courthouse last summer, my mother with cash in hand to pay for her car registration and tags, looking warm and wearied, like she felt the weight of the monotonous tasks of adult life.

Shirley punches the keypad next to the metal door and we're off and walking down a skinny corridor with Shirley leading the way; she has a slight limp.

"Post-polio syndrome," she says, turning back to me and pointing to her left leg, which is a mystery beneath her voluminous pants. She gives me a big smile.

I smile back and offer up a *Post-polio syndrome! Well,*

what are you gonna do? shrug. The smell of hot metal makes me think of life in an iron lung, and I'm starting to lose my nerve. But then a middle-aged couple in matching kelly-green sweat suits jostle past us and in unison say, "Thank God it's Friday!"

"You two have a good night," Shirley tells them, "and don't do anything I wouldn't do!" It's as if we are at a random block party, not a narrow hallway where the couple could take guns from their Jack and Jill leather bags—his blue, hers baby pink—and blow our heads off. The social contract of the pistol range involves a great deal of trust.

"Here we go," Shirley says. She leads me into a Plexiglas stall and clamps a pair of headphones over her ears, then hands me a pair. "Dang things squish my hair down," she says. I nod. Then it's a pair of safety goggles for her and for me, and the spent-bullet smell of smoke and gunpowder. Tears sting my eyes behind my safety goggles. Because the pistol range smells like a soldering iron touching metal, like the airless room at the Parks and Rec center where my mother and I took a stained-glass class when I was ten. The class was on Wednesday afternoon and my stomach always hurt from the long day at school, from Caitlin P. and Kendra J. hating my hair, but soon came the smell of hot metal, the soothing voice of the pantsuited retiree who taught the class. We made a wall hanging of a clutch of pink and purple pansies, the bright candy-colored glass encased in metal petals. My mother found it relaxing too; she loved the moment where the soldering iron touched the metal rings and the heat turned the metal rings to nougat.

Shirley hands me another clipboard, and I fill out yet another form, with my safety goggles on, as if I am in chemistry class. Shirley explains to me that once she loads the pistol, I am to point it away from my body and her body at all times, and that I need to concentrate, that I need to pay attention. Once she takes the safety off, I need to be both focused and relaxed as I aim at the target.

Focused and relaxed: a tricky oxymoron. But I will try, God knows I will try.

Shirley turns and looks out beyond the Plexiglas. Like in a bowling alley, the expanse is a long, skinny rectangle, except unlike in a bowling alley, there is a paper target with the outline of a body at the end.

She hands me the gun and it's so much heavier than my own pink and cream one. She shows me how to hold it and how to position my shoulders to account for the weight of it; she tells me how the gun will kick a little when it is fired, and that I need to hold it steady and stay calm and *pay attention pay attention pay attention.*

Which is not a problem for a girl like me.

I hold my rented gun—snub nosed, black with copper flourishes—and yes, I'm amazed: last year at this time it was my mother and I, our regular life of school and work and cooking and errands and planning our year in Europe. On Monday morning it was all "Welcome to the week, people, please try to finish *War and Peace* for the quiz on Tuesday," and by Friday night it's shooting ranges. By Friday it's me studying the paper target—the outline of a man wearing a suit—before I slowly pull the trigger, my forefingers flexing slowly, slowly, unsure of how much pressure is needed to make it happen. By Friday it's Shirley letting loose with a low whistle the first time I fire the gun and rip the radiant center of the paper target, the circular black heart. I feel the shot radiate inside me, shocking my sore rib. I get my latent asskisser's thrill from Shirley's approval. "You're a natural, girl."

And so I have talent for this. I shoot for fifteen minutes—it's best to keep it short the first time—and then it's a flurry of signing papers to give the gun back to Shirley, and her telling me to sign up for the classes, and giving me her pink business card embossed with a gun and a chrysanthemum and fancy font: *Shirley Campbell-Price, Range Master*. And it's good to know that I have a talent for this. Even though I don't think I'll need more than the one class, now I know that I could do it, can do it, would do it, will do it, the verbs so close to my heart.

And so it's all smiley thanks to Shirley Campbell-Price and of course I'll be back and bye-bye now as I drive off through the new snow—a girl with a new skill set, my mouth set in the harshest dog smile, so dry that my top lip hooks on my gums—to Woodrow Wilson High School.

* * *

So many lost moments! My mind in OCD overdrive as I cruise down the highway. So many times I could have said something! I think of seeing Alecia and her mother at Target, how her mother said that Catherine Bennett was "tough but good!" Why didn't I turn to her and ask, "Are you on crack, my good lady?"

Alecia's misguided mother.

In the cart, she had a package of Blendy pens tucked under a box of Cheerios, and I thought that later she might surprise Alecia, maybe tuck the pens under her pillow or put them in a craft cabinet, where Alecia would randomly find them and shriek in delight. But what good was her mother's kindness if she was going to be so duped? Did she not have an ounce of intuition, a bit of motherfucking horse sense?

And, for that matter, why didn't I tell my own mother how Mrs. Bennett treated Alecia when I had the chance? In that dreamworld chasm between the first day of school and the day my mother was killed? Because I could see it on the first day of class, Mrs. Bennett's peculiar interest, her savage joking: "Alecia! Sit right here! Alecia, I'll have to keep my eye on you, won't I?"

My mother hated a bully more than anything; surely she would have been outraged by Mrs. Bennett's behavior. My mother would have told Alecia's mother. My mother would have done something to help. Wouldn't she? Do something? Have done something?

The sadness of tense yet again as I turn into the student parking lot at Woodrow Wilson, hoping there are a few cars, a few people meeting up before they head out into the night. But the parking lot is dead, there's nothing and nobody, no weed-smokin' stragglers, there's just me, suddenly missing my locker, remembering things I left behind in that metal tomb. In my mind's eye I open my locker—right, 11; left, 14;

right, 8—and see a bruised banana on the top shelf drawing gnats in the marshy semidarkness, a tube of hair gel, chocolate-brown eyeliner, a Diet Coke, a stack of random school papers, and in the rectangular heart of my locker is a black boiled-wool cardigan from the sixties, and a soft, fabric-covered book that is my journal for English class, my history book, a heart-shaped mirror with a sticker that says WHO YOU LOOKIN' AT?

It's the journal that gets me, the journal my mother made for my birthday, a journal that involved a trip to the heirloom fabric store—a print of red Lenten roses, a blank journal purchased at the dollar store, and a glue gun. In the cold car I close my eyes and hear the sweet *shear-shear-shear* of her sewing scissors cutting the fabric, and my insides feel warmed and softened, and so I sit with my caramelized heart and my chilly hands on the steering wheel before I open the glove box.

I take out my gun. I tap it against my window. And look out at the school. Surely they must be wondering where I am. Not overly concerned, that much I know. But in the way of passively waiting: *Will Sandinista ever come back to school? Is she going to tell anyone this happened? Did the teacher hurt Sandinista when she kicked her desk?* Of course, the only adult who knows anything about that is Mrs. Bennett herself, and my guess is she isn't terribly worried about my welfare.

I push the mouth of my gun into the passenger seat for a second. It leaves a soft oval indentation on the gray fabric. I do it again. The fabric is mottled with stains and spills: lipstick, coffee, blue pen, carrot-ginger soup, strawberry smoothie. My mother longed for leather; she rued the thrift of the car's original owner.

Even though the gun is unloaded, the bullets safe in their box in the glove compartment, I imagine the gun accidentally going off, how it would give the wrong impression.

The school would be sweetly official: *Sandinista has a record of skipping school, so we weren't terribly concerned when she missed a week.* And here the school would be correct, because my mother had a loose policy about school attendance, her thought being that if she homeschooled me, I would never have to go to school, so what was so wrong about a girl taking a day off to go to the museum, or to read J. D. Salinger's *Nine Stories,* or to go for a hike during September's monarch migration? Plus, the school would have a pretty big out: *Her mother died in the fall. Naturally she was upset. Apparently she never recovered.* All the while relief warming the duplicitous bastards like whiskey straight from the bottle. Ahhh, in front of a bonfire on a winter night: *Now she won't complain. Not that she mattered. But still, now we are in the clear. That warms the old bones! Such a troubled girl, such bad luck! Well, maybe she's in a better place.*

Ha! Go fuck yourselves. I'd never do it.

My mother told me each and every night of my life: "There will never be anyone more precious to me than you, Sandinista. I love you more than anyone in the universe." The saccharine burden of it annoyed me.

I pop my gun back into the glove box. *I love you more than anyone in the universe.* I put on fresh lipstick—a matte brown-pink called Ashes of Roses—and press my lips together. I give myself a crazy smile in the rearview mirror to check for lipstick tracks. I clear my throat as if I'm about to make a speech. *I love you more than anyone in the universe.*

And then I drive home, slowly and carefully, as if I'm a chubby suburban mom in sweatpants driving a van with a Baby on Board sign in the window; over the icy patches I go, slowly and surely, as if I'm worth being saved.

saturday
GOD'S GUIDE TO GETTIN' IT ON

Saturday used to be the best day. My mom and I would go for pancakes and heavily creamed coffee at the diner, and then we would hit the thrift stores, the library for travel books, the grocery stores, a matinee, maybe popcorn and pie for dinner, sometimes a fancy dinner—my mother tying on her red and orange Ugandan apron and making pad thai and lemongrass soup, and then having friends over for Scrabble or going out into the night for more adventure, a concert, a drive under the stars. It was always the longest day, the most packed day of adventure, of the pure pleasure of no work or school, a day so reliably lovely that it would always inspire the Sunday blues.

But. Good-bye to all that.

Stepping out of my car on Thirty-Eighth Street, I have the jittery, dirt-gray feeling of no sleep and no phone calls and too many cigarettes. But at least I have the solace of work, if work is a candied shop with gleaming oak floors and racks of lovely clothes. And of course there is Bradley, Bradley taking the money, Bradley judiciously mocking those and *only* those who severely deserve it, Bradley who is reliably kind to the polite, to the downtrodden. And he has a lot of work to do, too, what with being the unwitting juxtaposition for the doom of my unringing phone, that seismic quiet, for Catherine Bennett, and for my whorl of pink-gun thoughts. My perpetual *Oh! What's a girl to do, what's a girl to do!* Well, to answer my own question, I suppose I could pay attention; I could sit up straight and listen carefully. I could look all the shining and heavily deluded people of this world in the eye and smile!

And now I am the proud owner of this brilliant little epiphany, which really should have been clear from the onset to anyone with a pulse: I know the school will not call. And it burns burns burns, but still I have something. I think of the words highlighted in my mother's white leatherette Bible from St. Scholastica's: *I will not leave you comfortless; I will come to you.*

Because I have a gun in my glove box, and my eyes are open, people, open, though weighted with heavy mascara, my long lashes fluttering like texturized spider legs. I wear a short skirt with irregularly spaced pear-green squares and arrows on a creamy tweed background, a black mohair sweater with a keyhole neckline (the black camisole beneath rescuing me from hoochie territory), black opaque tights and some big-ass shoes: four-inch platforms that give me the buoyancy of a moonwalker and pinch my baby toes, those poor little piggies that went wee wee wee all the way home.

The shop is busy—Saturday busy—which means no lunch hour, which means just Bradley zipping out the back for weed patrol and me eating a few poisoned circus peanuts before I smoke a cigarette out front. Henry Charbonneau is driving through obscure towns, hitting the estate sales with his new lovah, so this Saturday is just Bradley and me and the Pale Circus makes three. And despite my bleak week there are moments of real happiness: listening to Bradley hum *John Henry was a steel-drivin' man* as he rings up a studded leather jacket; watching a gray-haired woman bring her hand fluttering to her neck with delight when she steps out of the dressing room in a violet-blue cocktail dress she swore would make her look just ridiculous.

But always there is the metal shell of my dread, my heart a bronzed baby bootie of *fuck me fuck me fuck me.*

By afternoon I lose my resolve to be cool and realistic; I lose my vibe of *the school will not call and that is okay, or, that it really is not okay at all, but like many a morning gin drinker, God has granted me the knowledge to know the difference between what I can change and what I cannot change or whatever that alcoholic wisdom is.*

A girl with an auburn bob tries on a dove-gray dress with a fitted bodice that flares into layers and layers of moth-eaten tulle buoyed by a crinoline. When she looks at herself in the three-way mirror it is with pleasure, her eyes widening slowly, as if to modestly say: *Well, now. Wow.* She smiles.

Her teeth are the ruined oyster gray of a bulimic, and I am sad to see that she is a cutter, sad to see the thin raised scars striping her calves and inner arms.

Bradley is squatted down, straightening shoes so that they are equally spaced. He looks up at the girl in the gray dress and says, "Oh, that is great on you. Just great." And it's the second heartfelt *great* that gets us both—the girl looks stricken and I know for sure that his kindness is doing something to my own heart, trying to tamp down both my sorrow and my girl-with-the-gun-in-the-glove-box bravado. And so I wonder—and I can tell that the girl wonders too, her face private and pensive—can the semi-okay people of the earth not build some kind of army? Could we live in a commune, a cloister, protected from all the world is so quick to offer up?

My mind is hazy and soft, as if lined with toxic velveteen, and the hours, the hours, all the fucked-up or sublime hours, go too fast. Soon it is six o'clock and Bradley locks up and that's all there is, there isn't anymore—except for me wishing and wishing I had a cot in the back room.

I Windex and I clean the bathroom; I bag the trash and I straighten the racks, Swiffer the floor and dust the baseboards. Bradley does the cash register totals, his hand one with the calculator buttons as he adds up the checks, little pastel flags zipping between his fingers. He looks up at me and says, "Are you doing anything tonight?"

"'Washing my hair,' she said coquettishly." I twirl the feather duster in my hands, a peacock's swishing tail of silver and black and cobalt blue.

Instead of laughing Bradley merely gives me a rueful little smile.

I shrug. "I never do anything. Why?"

"I need a hit."

"Really?" I say. "Thinking of . . . a hit of . . . *moi*?" I twirl the feather duster again, but this time it is quite lame, a forced and awkward gesture.

"Yeah, baby," he says, plunging an imaginary hypodermic needle into the crook of his arm while making Bambi eyes at me.

"You'll have to try something in a different vein, no pun intended. I'm not interested in a shopgirl romance."

Bradley smiles but there is something dry and tired about our shopgirl humor, the jokey facade. The backbone of our forced humor is shrinking away, an osteoporosis of good cheer. I move the duster over the cash desk, over the cash register.

"I need my Jesus-hit."

"Oh."

Bradley rubber-bands the checks; he puts them in the bank bag with the cash. Henry Charbonneau will go to the bank first thing Monday morning; Henry Charbonneau is the moneyman.

"I know it's weird to ask someone to go to church with you, it's all evangelical and shit. Just so you know: I don't even believe in God. I'm a cultural Catholic to the extreme."

I steal a look at the crucifix tattoo on his thumb. *That's a lot of culture,* I think.

"But if you're not doing anything else tonight—"

"Bradley, I'm not. I never do anything."

Bradley locks the doors of the Pale Circus and we are out into the world, which has the cold, stinging look of *Hey, Mom, I think it's going to snow.* That old hurtful dreamscape. I daydream a brighter snow day, a snow day where the children laugh and play and Frosty does not melt away, where the mothers live forever and where there is hot chocolate and warm shortbread and the hard-assed individuality of snowflakes, their ephemeral pronged crystals.

Except I know that Catherine Bennett would ruin the snowy dreamscape of winter wonderland, that she would appear in her beige snow boots and nylon parka and yell out to Alecia Hardaway, *Alecia, yoo-hoo! Alecia! What is the substance that comes from the sky? It rhymes with "toe"!* And there would be Alecia in a striped stocking cap sprouting a festive tassel. She would be squinting as the snowflakes landed on her face. Alecia would knit her holly-green gloved hands together and try to puzzle it out.

I feel more mentally ill than usual and realize that I've had nothing but coffee, cigarettes and germy candy for the past twenty-four hours, that I'm not only internally jittery but physically trembling. When Bradley asks if he can drive—well, precisely what he says is "I'm good to drive," with a solemn nod—I am grateful to get in on the passenger side, to have a different point of view.

Mostly I like to be the person who is not in charge.

And so Bradley drives, and the car heater kicks on, and I am warm and sleepy, traveling with a safe person. I close my eyes and have the fantasy that Bradley is an escaped convict who is kidnapping me, and how completely, completely great that would be: Route 66, diners with strawberry malts and fat, crisp onion rings, motels with flamingos and vinyl lounge chairs arranged in a listless pattern around drained swimming pools, a homicidal front-desk clerk with a lazy eye working crossword puzzles. It would be entirely preferable to summer vacation, to burned noses and the hot, webbed plastic of the lounge chairs biting our bare calves. Bradley and I would sit in our winter coats by the empty pool, reading and daydreaming and smoking, watching the snow fall.

But wait, look who's ruining our bliss: there stands Catherine Bennett at the outdoor vending machine, wiggling her dollar bill into the silver slot, working hard for a stale Mars Bar.

I must doze off for five full minutes or more, because when I open my eyes, we are off the interstate and driving slowly through Mission Hills, an old-money suburb with Tudor houses sweet as fairy-tale castles. When I watch a black Lab being chased through a snowy yard by happy doll-children in colorful ski gear, I'm disgusted and envious.

"This neighborhood is really lovely, in a completely bourgeois way," I say. "It shows how capitalism works beautifully for the top tier of society." The words just pop out, and I realize this is precisely the freelance social commentary my mother indulged in: basically correct, though vexingly self-righteous.

"Thanks." Bradley chuckles.

"What?"

He drives a half block and then points to a cream and red brick Tudor on the left. "That's my house."

"Oh, my God!" We both crack up at my faux pas. I wonder, though, about Bradley: he seems not just a mere college guy home from the dorm, enjoying the aesthetic pleasures—I imagine a library inside, a stone fireplace, many a built-in walnut bookcase—in his family home.

The snow starts again, a breezy powder on the windshield fine as baker's sugar. When I squint, I see my mother lying on her stomach on the hood of the car. With her chin resting on one hand and her feet crossed, she looks as casual as if she is stretched out on the living room floor watching TV. My mother smiles at me, snow glittering her dark hair, the briefest veil of diamonds.

The Clash song "Train in Vain" comes on the radio, and Bradley says, "Sooo, Sandinista, tell me, do you feel a spiritual connection to Joe Strummer? Since your mom clearly picked the name for a reason and probably not just because she liked the song, but . . . wait!" He turns and does a dramatic double take.

In Darth Vader's breathy evil voice he says, "Sandinista, Joe Strummer is your father."

"Nope," I say. "I mean, he *could* be, for all I know. But since Joe Strummer is dead, it's kind of a losing deal either way."

"Right," he says. He glances in the rearview mirror, looking troubled by this new information. "I kind of wondered, just being at your house. I didn't see any pictures of men—"

"Does Johnny Depp not count? Did you not see the vintage 21 *Jump Street* poster on the back of my door?"

"Oh, he counts; he counts double."

As we pull up in front of Our Lady of the Immaculate Conception—my mother called it Our Lady of Mercedes—it seems that I might be inherently Catholic, because I am more than a little okay with the whole idea of an immaculate conception, of holy sperm and egg scrambled in that great petri dish in the sky—it is, in fact, my preference to the idea of my mother hooking up with a guy at a Cure concert.

Bradley is making a sharp right into the church parking lot and I am sad to be done sailing along the snowy streets, but here we are: the steeple shooting up into the gray sky, the tasteful red brick, the arched windows covered with a milky gray substance. All around us families are getting out of their SUVs and sparkling charcoal-gray wagons, a tableau of shiny swinging hair and dark wool coats and gleaming teeth. Everyone is white. If not for the upscale vibe, it could be a Ku Klux Klan rally. The Catholic church in my neighborhood is Our Lady of Guadalupe, so I am not used to this sea of white Catholics slip-sliding across the parking lot. They grab hands like strings of cut-paper dolls before they take hold of the handrail and parade up the stone steps.

I think of my mother abandoning her principle of *Give No Money to the World's Most Corrupt Corporation* by buying tamales and fanciful dolls at the Our Lady of Guadalupe Fiesta each summer, how she would dance in the church parking lot with the believers, beautiful in her embroidered

Guatemalan dress and espadrilles, hands flashing over her head.

The lump in my throat is more like a goiter.

And Catherine Bennett asks if I am paying attention and my mind goes sour and swirling and why, oh why, were the only calls I received this week from telemarketers and an alcoholic looking for her beloved guinea pig? Why is my mother dead? And every grief is mine, but then there is the pleasure of another person, the pleasure of Bradley sitting next to me in the front seat, a rueful little grin on his face as he finally finds a parking spot.

Bradley takes the key out of the ignition and says, "My parents got married at this church."

"Yeah?" What I decide not to say—infected as I suddenly am by my mother's lefty sarcasm—is *Your parents got married at Our Lady of Mercedes? Kick-ass!*

"My dad loves to tell the story: they did their premarital counseling with this sort of deluded middle-aged priest who tried to give them sexy advice about the wedding night."

"Yuck! Ack!"

"Because who is the priest to say, right?"

"Uh, yeah, like, did he read *God's Guide to Gettin' It On* and share the knowledge?"

Bradley rewards me with a crescendo of sudden, snorting laughter. The snow starts falling in earnest, covering the windshield in a fast, flecked pattern, and I think of a white cotton dress my mother made me when I was in kindergarten. The dress had demure raised polka dots. *Dotted Swiss,* my mother told me, and in memory those words come out of her mouth slowly, the last *S* soft and lingering. The car fills with the hot electrical smell of her old Singer sewing machine.

Bradley laughs a final time. "The priest told my parents not to be nervous, not to worry, that it is a shocking thing for everyone to encounter for the first time."

"And . . . again, he would know . . . because?"

"Exactly. And so my parents were stuck in his hot little office that smelled like beer and feet, trying hard not to laugh about his assumptions of their virginity, because as my mom says, 'This was the early eighties and everyone liked to "party."'" Bradley does one of Henry Charbonneau's finger-hooks around the word *party* and shudders.

I cringe, empathetic. "One time my mom was describing this old boyfriend and she said, 'He was a very *giving* lover.'"

"How very enriching for you to know such an intimate thing about your mother's *lovah*," Bradley says. "Truly, there are things we are not meant to know. Anyhow, the priest finally tells my parents, these two eighties kids who have 'partied' a lot, that if they become anxious about consummating their love, they should remember one very important thing: the King of Kings will be there with you, *all* night long."

"Oh God!" I make many a retching sound. "Jesus in the boudoir? Is he lighting incense?" I do my best *To Sir, With Love* cockney accent: "Tell me, love, is the savior wearing silky knickers?'"

"Right? And so my mom is about to implode with laughter, when my dad looks at the priest and says, 'Well, Padre, in the words of the great Oscar Wilde: In bed, two's company, three's a crowd.'"

"Did he die? Did the priest fall down and die?"

"I don't know. Dad's always pissing himself by the time he gets to the punch line." Bradley nods up at the church. "Shall we?"

"Well," I say, feeling nervous now that we are actually at church, my performance anxiety kicking in. "I'm not actually Catholic."

"That's okay! I mean it's actually preferable, I would think."

"My grandparents were Catholic. They died when I was in junior high. When I was little they lived in Florida, and when I visited them during the summers and at Christmas they always took me to their church: St. Mary, Star of the Sea."

Bradley smiles sadly, gives a knowing nod, because of course he shares my aesthetic sense and is envisioning the Mother of Christ breaking the waves, her slick black hair braided with seaweed and shells. And of course I think of my own mother, of all the beautiful ladies lost at sea.

"And my mom was Catholic . . . earlier in her life . . . when she was in school, when she was a child. She went to St. Scholastica's, the whole deal. But she was sort of *way* not into it by the time I came along. Excessively not into it."

"Yeah," Bradley says. "That can happen."

"She didn't want me to go to a Catholic school—I guess some weird things happened at St. Scholastica's in the eighties. She was all like, 'You need to go to a public school where there's some goddamn accountability, where they don't sweep all the crazy shit under the rug.'"

Bradley winces.

"I know, right? See also: overblown irony. See also: Catherine Bennett. See also: Sandinista Jones. Thanks, Mom."

"It's like the assholes are everywhere. The assholes have the power. The assholes with their lame advice, their pompous lectures. The assholes who never apologize. No matter what you do, no matter where you go." When Bradley starts to blink, it's more like a tic. "You cannot outrun them."

I feel a little panicked that he's going to start crying. My mother taking me to the Unitarian church with the poster that said FEELINGS ARE NEITHER GOOD NOR BAD, THEY JUST ARE! was a big waste of time. Apparently I am some kind of android who fears all human emotion. I don't know why I hate to see a boy cry, why it's such a knife.

"But I'm happy to be going with you," I say quickly. "I mean, I haven't been to any kind of church in ages and ages. Probably the sight of me will surprise and disgust Jesus Christ in equal measure. Jesus will float down and vomit on my dress because I'm such a whorish hoodlum and all. Plus I smoke crack and worship the devil on alternate Thursdays."

And it works, my lame humor works, just a little: Bradley smiles.

"And I think it'll be really interesting to go to Mass with you."

Bradley sighs. "Yeah . . . yep. I guess it'll be that if nothing else."

And then we get out of my car like any other couple and walk through the snowy parking lot. As I button my coat—trying to look proper and all despite my platform shoes—I slip on the slick curb and Bradley reaches for my hand. Then we go up the marble steps, rock salt scritching beneath our shoes. When we pull open the front doors to the vestibule we are greeted by a stone Virgin Mary holding a font of holy water. Bradley dips his fingers in her bowl and makes the sign of the cross—forehead, heart, shoulder, shoulder—and we enter the next set of doors.

Inside the church it is a continent of stained glass, an aisle of deep blue carpet splitting the rows of polished mahogany pews in two clean halves: BC and AD, the bride's side, the groom's side. On the altar is an old-school crucified Jesus—no contemporary look of neutral sadness at having to die for our sins for *this* particular Son of God. He is not having it. His mouth has gone slack with agony, his carved eyebrows draw together in dramatic perplexity: *WTF?*

Flanking the altar are carved saints staring me down with their moon marble eyes, and to the left is a separate little altar for Mary, resplendent in her standard-issue baby-blue robe, bouquets of red roses at her feet.

The church is quiet, save for some pleasant infant babbling, and warm with the smells of candle wax and spent roses. A tiny, ancient nun in a street-length black dress, short habit and Birkenstocks welcomes me, a hand on my back, a plain, pale mouth saying "Good evening, thank you for joining us." And I certainly understand why people would sign on to marry Jesus, to rest in this perfumed eucharistic high without the normal worries of STDs or the Guy Who Doesn't Call You Back.

And so it is my pleasure to shake the nun's hand; it's my pleasure to follow Bradley into Our Lady of the Immaculate Conception, to have the feeling of belonging to something and someone. Bradley bends deeply on one knee at the end of a pew toward the back, and I do a slight dip too, a sort of church curtsy, and then I sit beside him. He pulls down the cushioned kneeler and kneels. I stay seated and take a long look around—the beautiful elderly couple in front of me, a frail old doll in a red wool coat with a fox collar, her skeletal husband looking starched and nautical in pinstripes and a blue blazer. A beefy-looking Irishman with weedy eyebrows sits down next to me, the flash of smile before he kneels, like Bradley, to pray. On the other side of Bradley is a family with three little girls decked out in zebra-print jumpers and black patent-leather Mary Janes with matching purses. The mother absently strokes the middle girl's hair; the littlest girl eats Cheerios out of a plastic purple tub patterned with princesses.

I feel at peace.

Everything feels so holy and real to me, though, according to my mother, all of Catholicism is a beautiful enigma wrapped in a layer of bullshit, stuffed inside a layer of abuse. Still, the inside of this church is so pleasing—I run my hand over the polished roses and crosses carved into the pew, over the soft leather choir book with the word *missalette* stamped in faded, flaking silver. To be sure, Our Lady of the Immaculate Conception is pure loveliness. It is the Pale

Circus of churches, so undoubtedly there are a few rats, but it's so hard not to feel stoned on the physical beauty of it all.

Mass starts with a blast of organ from the front of the church and, without warning, French horns and a trumpet from the choir loft. Viva Las Vegas! But then a beautiful white-robed altar girl starts down the aisle, grinning and embarrassed, holding a brick-red Bible aloft over her head. Behind her is an altar boy, and then the priest, singing out of his missalette. And then there's a smorgasbord of sitting and standing, and singing while kneeling on the padded kneelers, and altar boys and girls floating around the altar in their angel clothes. The first two Bible readings are done by a regular guy in a suit—he appears to be a *lay*person (here, my brain cooks up some junior high fun: a person who gets *laid!*), but then the priest goes to the podium on the altar. He takes a dramatic pause, and says, "A reading from the gospel according to Matthew."

Bradley makes a little cross over his forehead, lips and heart—I look around and everyone is doing this, and it's all sort of sort of sexy/creepy but nonetheless fascinating, and I realize that I have not thought about the whole Catherine Bennett debacle since I stepped into Our Lady of the Immaculate Conception.

But of course noting this simultaneously ruins my peace and I'm now thinking about all of it, the school and Mrs. Bennett and no one calling, and I am not *paying attention,* the gospel according to Matthew is completely lost to me.

But the handsome priest, a tall dishwater blond with bangs falling into his eyes and a square jawline, steps away from the podium on the altar. The priest wears a red cassock. I know this garment is called a cassock thanks to Honors English III, thanks to Ms. Lisa Kaplansky, lover of Leo Tolstoy's "Father Sergius."

Lisa Kaplansky, Lisa Kaplansky.

When I look over at Bradley, I see that he has his own sorrows, I see that he is chewing his thumbnail, the cross tattoo on his thumb pressed to his mouth.

I lean in close and assume a serious expression, as if about to enquire about last rites or fire exits. Bradley smells sporty and clean, like men's deodorant. "I love the priest's flaming-red dress," I whisper. "I think somebody's in possession of a Big Bad Wolf obsession."

I would like to make Bradley laugh out loud in church, to see him dip his head and double over. But he only fake-smiles, his lips drawn tightly over teeth.

The priest walks to the front of the church, his red cassock swishing behind him, the bloodied bride of Christ, and he speaks casually, as if hosting a game show or giving an impromptu dinner-table soliloquy.

"When I was growing up, the Feast of the Epiphany was traditionally the day we took down our Christmas decorations. My family was always a little crabby that day. I remember one year the tree tipped over, the glass ornaments broke—little shards everywhere—the brown shag carpet in our family room was a minefield and all of us kids learned some new words from my father."

Raucous laughter from the pews, the choir loft: the parishioners at Our Lady of the Immaculate Conception have never heard anything so exquisitely hilarious. I try to give Bradley a secretive eye roll, but he is completely focused on the priest. And Bradley is not laughing; he's not even smirking.

The priest collects his praise, smiling, before he starts again. "Now, *epiphany* comes from the Greek *epi phanos,* which means 'to appear.' We tend to think of the Feast of the Epiphany in terms of the wise men, the magi, making their dangerous journey to come and adore the baby Jesus, who of course is the promise of our salvation, the word made flesh. But the real Feast of the Epiphany is not just for the wise men, but for each of us, every day. Christ wants to be seen, to be loved, like we all do. He came to us a human being who had to submit completely to the joys and terrors of a human life, as a baby who would be wrapped in swaddling and worshipped, an adult who would be stripped of his garments and nailed to a cross."

And here amid the lushness of the candled altar, the dark pews, the deep red roses placed at the feet of the Virgin Mary, the little girls in festive wintry dresses, and the smell of incense and candle wax, Catherine Bennett's wild paisley slip floats down from the choir loft. I look up and watch it shimmy in the air like a drunken, multicolored bird. It floats in my peripheral vision all through Mass, until the priest tells us all to offer one another a sign of peace.

Bradley gives me an earnest hug and I close my eyes, and, just like that, the slip disappears. I shake hands with the elderly couple in front of us—the old lady's bony hand feels frail and hollow, the veins like pipe cleaners—and I shake hands with the beefy Irishman and everyone says "Peace be with you, peace be with you, peace be with you," . . . and it works, just a little. The sensation of someone offering you a bit of salve, the formal anesthesia of kindness—peace be with you, peace be with you, peace be with you—blinds your neurons a bit, so your situation does not feel quite as grave.

The organ starts up, and, following Bradley's lead, I kneel on the padded kneeler. Prayers and more prayers. On the altar, the priest pours an ominous pink liquid—blood of Christ? vino?—from a glass decanter into a goblet. He holds a golden dish in his palms and says, *Take this, all of you, and eat it.* I think of Erika shaking the Comet into the bowl of frosting, how there are so many ways to give and receive Communion. But then it's time to pay attention! Three lines of people snake up to the front of the altar, with ancient men in rayon sport shirts directing traffic at the end of the pews. People descend from the choir loft and filter into the established lines. The priest stands in front of the altar with a golden dish, his helpers with their little golden dishes at his side. Bradley appears to be in some fugue state of anguish, his face gone tense and masklike. And then we're off to the altar; it's our pew's turn to take Communion, and when everyone stands up, I do too.

I've never had a First Communion, never held my mouth open for the Savior, but I figure that a kindhearted Jesus would not want me to wait in the pew, a Mass wallflower. Mostly what I think is: *When in Rome . . .*

I have learned about Catholicism through my mother's

complaining and through the books of her childhood, but I wish I had paid a little more attention when I went to Mass with my grandparents in Florida when I was little. My mother would stay at their condo to drink coffee and read the paper, enjoying what she jovially referred to as her sacrament-free Sunday. My grandmother would always have a new dress for me, and I have the memory of staying in the pew at St. Mary, Star of the Sea, during Communion, of staring at the embroidered sand dollars on my sundress while everyone else accepted the body of Christ.

But for all anyone in this church knows, my mother was a religious fanatic; no one knows that I am not a Catholic. And so with Bradley in front of me and the Irishman with weedy eyebrows behind me, I feel cosseted and protected as I walk to the front of the church, like no one can hurt me here in Jesusville. I have what I imagine to be a bridal feeling of happiness—of imminent change—right before I notice something is wrong with Bradley. We are packed in close, just inches between our bodies, so I notice that beneath his white broadcloth shirt—Bradley changed out of his Spanktones vintage T before we left the Pale Circus—his shoulders are moving up and down too fast, as if he is having an asthma attack. But it's too late to turn back now; we're the next in line. I watch over Bradley's shoulder as the priest holds up the Eucharist wafer between his thumb and forefinger and says: "The body of Christ." Each syllable has its own weight. Bradley makes a basket out of his hands and he says something under his breath that I can't quite catch. The priest lays the wafer in Bradley's hands, and then it's my turn.

The priest looks at me, holds up the wafer—which I see up close is bone-colored, though I assumed it would be a bleached-wheat snow-white. The priest says the same thing he said to Bradley: "The body of Christ."

I wonder if he tires of saying that so many times, if the priest ever has the urge to hold up the wafer and burst out with some random sentence: *After all, you're just another brick in the wall. Top o' the morning, my little chickadee. Kiwi fruit is seeded and delicious.* Mostly what I am wondering is what I should say, because there are a zillion people behind me in line, and I cup my empty hands.

The priest repeats his words, softly: "The body of Christ." Clearly I have to sing for my supper here, so I smile up at him. I nod and whisper, "Okay. Thanks so much."

He surprises me by breaking out with a big smile that looks non-holy and real, and he puts the Eucharist wafer in my hands. I pop it in my mouth and I think how well this is all going, the priest's smile warming me. I have the random thought that going to Mass might make me feel a lot better and that maybe I will start taking the classes or whatever to get officially signed up.

There is a bottleneck of people around the altar, all us pilgrims who have taken the body of Christ from the nice priest are waiting for his blood, which is served not by the priest, but by the laypeople. As I am a fan of Anne Rice and in possession of an inner goth girl, I feel very chipper about phase two of Holy Communion: a woman to the left of the altar in a taupe pantsuit and kitten heels holds up a gold goblet to each person, and after they drink, she wipes the lip of the goblet with a white cloth. I feel happy to wait in line behind Bradley, to have a dry circular biscuit stuck to the roof of my mouth. Yes, it's the body of Christ—but what part? His tonsils? His soft, infected gumline? Maybe I will bite down on the wafer and feel the bird-bone crunch of his seventh vertebra: Now, *that's* good eatin'.

But in truth I start to go all Christ-crazy and I think: *What if it could be true, what if the priest could really do such a fabulous, fabulous trick with flour and fermented grapes—with the body and the blood—and I feel it;* I feel my mind being slowly and firmly blown, and I think, *I am so going to take the Catholic classes.* Then I look at the carved statue of the Virgin Mary to the left of the altar, and it's my mother's face there, my mother forever trapped in that pale blue stone robe. My mom gives me an expansive eye roll, a lavish, sardonic smile, which means: *Get a grip, sister. I'd rather you be a Hare Krishna.*

And then the line moves—we are very close to getting our drink of blood/wine. I am mesmerized by the woman whisking the cloth over the goblet, the flash of her coral-pink nails against the gold and starched white. Though I've never scored better than a C-plus in biology, even I can tell that swiping a bit of cloth over the cup is not going to kill the germs. But maybe Christ sanitizes everything, his ghostly breath a spray of Purell on the lip of the goblet.

When there is only one person in front of him, Bradley cuts out of the wine line, his hands folded, his head bowed. I zip out of line and follow, sad to miss out on the vampire aesthetic, the sanguinary zinfandel. And I'm confused about the wafer: I can't remember if I'm supposed to chew or just swallow it whole. I'm pretty sure it's a faux pas to chew up the body of Christ like a mouthful of Pringles, so I just press my lips into a demure smile like a ventriloquist's doll—the word I believe is *dummy*—and decide to let the wafer melt on my tongue like an M&M.

But it doesn't melt; it adheres to the roof of my mouth like papier-mâché.

I have to walk fast to keep up with Bradley, he is race-walking down the side aisle, which seems a little rude, though who am I to say. I look ahead, scouting out our empty pew, and recognize it by my own purse and by the girly artifacts left behind by the family waiting in line for the blood of Christ—the headless Barbie, the tiny patent-leather purses, the sparkly notebooks and scattered crayons. But Bradley whisks right by our pew, not looking back to see if I am following. I grab my purse and hustle to catch up with him.

I'm gaining on him when I'm distracted by the enclosed glass room at the back of the church. I didn't notice the room when I entered Our Lady of Immaculate Conception. There is a carved mahogany sign over the door that says THE CRY ROOM. Every house should have one! I guess every house does. As I walk past, I see the brief tableau of infants and tired-looking mamas sitting in folding chairs, a toddler building a squat tower of blocks, his little fat hand reaching out to put a red block on an orange block. And then I reach the sweet spot at the back of the church, the double doors that lead to the vestibule, where the nun shakes your hand, where the brides and their fathers wait to take their long walk down the aisle.

The doors swing and squeak in Bradley's wake. When I catch the handle and pull open the door, I see that Bradley is storming the vestibule, tearing past a woman holding a baby. He pulls open the doors to the outside world, and Bradley leaves Our Lady of the Immaculate Conception.

As the woman bounces the baby on her hip, she gives me a sort of knowing look, as if I'd gotten into some whisper-fight with my beau at church, as if I'm trailing after him, re-pentant and misty-eyed. She hits me up with the old, knowing "Honey, all men are jackasses" smile.

I smile back at her, but in fact many ladies are jackasses too. I have noticed this phenomenon, people. I have most certainly paid attention. The baby squeals and the woman turns her attention to infant entertainment; she points to the stone statue of the Virgin by the doors and says, "Maaary, Maary." But the baby, a long-lashed dream in a fluffy violet jacket, appears unimpressed. She bucks her head back and squeals some more.

I look at the statue, and I see that this Mary does not be-long to the Precious Moments school of statuary; she does not have the plasticine look of gentle awe layered with re-signed wonder. To be sure, she does not have the sardonic, all-knowing expression of my own mother. This Mary looks searching, surprised, her granite brows drawn together so fiercely that no amount of Botox could turn back the clock. She appears to hold out her bowl of holy water with frantic animation: *Here! Take some! It's good!*

And her smile is all wrong, deeply carved dimples that do not match her panicky eyes. And so, cold air blowing in the door, I see that Our Lady of Immaculate Conception is no one if not Alecia Hardaway, perplexed but trying to be a good sport: *I'm going to be the mother of Jesus? I'm pregnant? What will this be like? I'm pregnant! Oh, good, I'm pregnant! But . . . what's* pregnant?

And Catherine Bennett appears next to the statue and screams into the stone swirl of her veil: *Pregnant means there is a fetus in your uterus! Alecia, Earth to Alecia! Do you know how you got pregnant? Was it the angel, Alecia? Did the angel bring you good news?*

The woman with the baby touches my arm and I give a little gasp. She smiles and puts a flyer in my hands. And then I am off into my secular twilight, going down the church steps in my perilous shoes, the ice-crusted railing giving my hand a little bite when I touch it, the cold air stinging my teeth.

I suppose it's better to be Bradley, incendiary, no fear of falling as he walks through the parking lot kicking up patches of snow that swirl and evanesce into blustery ghosts. The parking lot is quiet as a winter graveyard. My mother's headstone appears in my mind—HEATHER JONES—beneath a clutch of carved irises. That was my idea, my heavy touch. Mother had an iris bloom tattooed to her bicep. "'Iris' means wisdom," she told me, proudly peeling the adhesive tape away from the bandage to reveal a patch of blistered purple bloom. The tattoo artist had done a lovely job; it looked as if the real flower had been pressed below the surface of my mother's skin, as if it would glow there forever.

When Bradley finally reaches my car, he touches the passenger-door handle. He turns his head and stares absently at the Cadillac Escalade parked next to us before he tilts his head back and, with a *phifffft* sound that cuts the winter air, spits out the Lord: his Eucharist wafer sails up, buoyant, before landing silently on the hood of the Cadillac.

I walk through the slushy parking lot, my careful feet the only sound in the world. When I get closer, I see it: the grain-colored disk lodged on the snowy hood of the car.

Bradley is breathing hard and looking down at his feet. And so I have that bad moment of self-knowledge: aside from being ever so pure-hearted and persecuted, I am also a fairly big jackass. I am the self-involved collector of pain with no thoughts of Bradley's troubles. I am that super, super creepy person who corners you on the bus and tells you some random thing about his or her dysfunctional family, using the term *dysfunctional,* saying it right out loud, so as to be victimized again by the tacky TV-speak of it all.

I am the person who exists solely to suck up your pity and leave you no choice but to nervously exclaim: *Oh, my God! Oh, no! I just can't believe it!* As if everyone didn't have their own story. Stor*ies.*

Bradley gets in the car, slamming the door.

When I get in the car we sit in the silence, not admiring the lavender-gray twilight. We look down at the car mats. I read the flyer the woman gave me. It has the Mass schedule at Our Lady Of the Immaculate Conception for the upcoming week. With a flicker, the parking lights switch on.

I clear my throat. I do the girl thing, the mom thing, the über-Midwestern thing. I say: "Bradley. Hey! Do you maybe want to go for pancakes?" It comes out with a lisp, as *pacakth,* because of the wafer stuck to the roof of my mouth.

"Yes," he says gravely. "I do want to go for pancakes. Will you drive?"

We switch seats—the cold air startling us anew as we open our car doors. I readjust the mirrors, I get the heater going, vented warmth on our faces, and I'm putting the car in drive, when Bradley places his hand on mine. "Wait," he says.

I look over at him.

Bradley says: "The whole thing with Robert?" He says the name sweetly, wholesomely—Rahbert—as if it's a sparkling summer berry. "With," he says with a grimace, "Father Bob?"

I look down at the flyer and see his name in a fancy font: *Father Robert Dugan.*

"It started when I was fifteen."

"Oh, yeah?" I give up a fake-casual cough and cover my mouth with my hand; I stick my thumb in my mouth and scrape the Communion wafer from the roof of it. I put the remains in my coat pocket.

"I mean, it's not like I was *five.*"

I nod. I look down, as if in perpetual thrall to the grooved plastic lines in the car mats, the embedded pebbles and dirt clods. "Well. Five would be bad."

Bradley digs in his jacket pocket. "Do you mind?"

"Oh, God no! Please! Please." I make a whirling tornado of my hand. "Please go ahead."

Bradley unwinds his window a few inches. I crank the heat higher to compensate. He makes quick work of his rolling papers and weed. He fires up with his Zippo lighter and inhales the deepest breath, a "seven Chinese brothers swallowing the ocean" breath that makes the joint sizzle and burn bright orange.

Bradley's face is compressed agony as he holds in the smoke; his expression makes the grimace of the crucified Jesus look blasé: *Damn, I forgot my coupons.* When I see a tear on the plane of his cheek, I look down at my hands.

My mother's favorite book was *The Catcher in the Rye,* which I felt was such an obvious favorite book, a clichéd captain-of-the-football-team favorite book. She would often channel Holden Caulfield when she felt happy, saying: "There are a lot of nice things in the world. I mean, a lot of nice things. We're all such morons to get sidetracked." But both J. D. Salinger and my mother may have been wrong about this.

Bradley finally shudders and coughs out the smoke. He takes a violent swipe at his face, clearing the tears.

"I thought I would think about him less when I was away from him. All last summer I had the thought that, in the fall, when I was away at college, I would love him less, I would think about him less." Bradley gives a devil-may-care shrug, a cocky smile. "But, not so much." He takes another long drag. In the choked silence I stare up at Our Lady of the Immaculate Conception, at the stained-glass windows that are covered with the opaque gray substance. What the hell is it? An environmental treatment? Plasticine ashes? Covert sin?

"As it turns out, the whole love thing doesn't really leave because you will it to. I don't know what to do." Bradley inhales and holds it for as long as he can, until his shoulders shudder and he artfully exhales a long stream of smoke through the inch of unrolled space in the car window. "I have to just wait it out, wait for that day when I don't care anymore. I'm waiting to love him less, though that's happening pretty goddamn slowly, if at all. But I think letting someone go is like the Holy Spirit entering your heart: you can't make it happen, you just have to be *available* to it."

And I'm a little lost on the theology angle, mainly just thinking: *Love? Huh? Are you* kidding *me?*

"So, yeah, I guess so," I say, encouragingly, my voice fraught with faux casualness, with my *I'm so down with your relationship with the abusive priest* vibe. I nod excessively. What is there to say?

"Anyway, it's an old story, I know. I think the pedestrian aspect of it is what bothers me most." Bradley takes another long drag. "I went to Disneyland, and I got the Mickey Mouse ears. Although I didn't really understand that at the time."

This seems slightly rehearsed, but optimistic, as if he's wishing himself into a world where he will be free, a summation of heartache with an amusement-park analogy.

"So," I say, because it is apparently impossible for me to start a sentence without nodding and saying "so." And I'll be goddamned if I don't say it again with a nod that's verging on a perpetual head bobble. "So, wow—"

"I saw him last night. Here. It was a little better between us. . . . We smoked a lot and, you know . . . Usually when I see him now, it's just crazy. It's nothing. He's all formal and hearty: 'Hellooo, Bradley! Bradley, I hope you're studying and not going to too many keggers!'"

"Keggers? Who says 'keggers'? Does he think it's 1982?"

Bradley looks up at the church and over at the carriage house behind it, the same sweet Tudor-and-stone style as the church and Bradley's own home, just blocks away. This whole neighborhood so Hansel-and-Gretel quaint. I know that not only has Bradley been in the house, he probably knows the domestic mysteries of it, the hand towels, magazines and ottomans, the brand of dishwashing liquid next to the kitchen sink.

I try not to think about Bradley seeing Father Bob last night.

"None of it really matters, anyway. I've figured it out. He has someone new. His name is Miles. He was a couple years behind me in school. He comes from this super, super rich family that's trying to bring back the Latin Mass. So I feel bad for him . . . I guess. Miles. He's never going to be able to have the gay talk with his parents. You can tell they love their country club Christ more than any of their kids."

Anther brilliant comment from me: "Wow." It's the best I can do with all this new information, with my mind swirling with Father Bob and Bradley, Father Bob and Miles. *What animal should you never play cards with? A cheetah!*

The church door flings open and Father Bob appears, his cassock billowing out like a superhero cape as he leans down and fixes the doorstop.

Bradley takes a long last drag off his joint, then opens the car door and stuffs the stub into a short cliff of dirty snow. And then we sit in silence as we watch Father Bob, or as Bradley calls him, *Robert.* He folds his hands behind his back and looks up at the sky. Soon, people stream or straggle out of the church. Most everyone stops to chat with Father Bob, to shake his hand. He cups his hand over a little girl's head while he leans down to talk to her, then throws back his head and laughs.

Bradley sighs. "You know, the thing is, my parents are so goddamn nice, it's annoying. They've always tried so hard." He assumes a chirpy falsetto, approximating a mom's voice: "Bradley, you are always free to bring a love interest home for dinner or to play backgammon, I don't want you to feel any different than your brother would about bringing a girl home."

"Wow," I say. "That's totally nice." In truth, I had thought all Catholics were kind of jackassy about these matters.

"Although I'm not quite sure my mom would have been so thrilled had I shown up at home and said, 'Mom, waiting on the front porch is my very special date for the evening. We are deeply in love, so please don't freak out that he's older than I am. Oh, and one more thing, my special guy is none other than beloved Father Bob.'"

I laugh, thinking about this complicated game of Mystery Date. It's amazing that mothers, even kind and decent mothers, are so highly delusional. I remember my own mom at Target, yukking it up with Alecia Hardaway's mom over algebra teachers and playgroups. Their candied view seems so lame, but I suppose that mothers simply cannot know. My mind veers into grammatical confusion, and I correct myself; I let myself feel the pain of the singular, the punch of the past conditioned tense: *My mother simply could not have known.*

Bradley drums his fingers on the dashboard. "Shall we blow this Popsicle stand? This little old Eucharist-wafer shack?"

"Absolutely," I say. "I'm starving."

I manage to back out of the parking space, but the place is jumping with crazy Catholic drivers. They may have enjoyed Mass, but now they are definitely ready to get the hell out of here. I get stuck behind a jumble of cars. Bradley is looking out the window, watching Father Bob. I look up at the church and wonder again about the coating of gray on the stained-glass windows. Inside, the lit windows are so gorgeous, the robes of the saints glowingly root-beer brown, bottle green and velvet blue, their Cupid's bow mouths as jeweled and red as crushed rubies.

I point up at the windows. "What's the deal? Why can't you see the stained glass from the outside?"

Bradley looks up and says, "The church had to put a protective covering on them a few years back so they could get insurance."

I stare at the windows, inadvertently taking my foot off the brake and nearly hitting the Escalade that has pulled out in front of me, that big glimmering vehicle with the body of Christ clinging to the snowy hood.

"Shit!" I hit the brake just as the Escalade pulls up. "Why do they need insurance—"

"People used to break the windows at night. They threw rocks."

"Now, why would someone go and do a thing like that? Those windows are *art*." But I know how pleasing it is to hear glass break at night, to live in that half second before it falls into a cushion of snow. And to break the church windows? The shrieking saints, the clash of breaking glass, rainbow shards bleeding onto the asphalt below?

Bradley smiles. "I have not the faintest idea why someone would commit such a rogue act. It is a sorrowful mystery."

* * *

For our Saturday-night fun, we hit the International House of Pancakes; we are hopping at IHOP. We are starving to death and there is a thirty-minute wait, so we gorge on candy of unknown origins from the dirty dispensers next to the newspaper machines. By the time we're finally seated, the overheated restaurant has made us frantic with thirst. We drink up our short glasses of ice water so quickly that the waitress sets two more down in front of us with a scolding sigh, thinking we are on meth. And of course we are equally hungry for everything on the menu and we agonize over our decisions, staring at the shiny photographs of sunny-side-up eggs and hot chocolate topped with ivory whorls of whipped cream. In the end, I go with a huge-ass stack of pancakes topped with bright, canned strawberries. Bradley gets the blueberry crepes. We drink cup after cup of coffee—we have to! It's so weak once you grow accustomed to espresso.

And then we discover—via our sugared headaches—that a low-protein diet might make us even more mentally ill, so we very politely order a second meal of breakfast meats. The sausage is black and flaking from the grill and the bacon is severely undercooked, soft and curly blond at the edges. And yet still we stuff ourselves, the fried food a change of pace from the usual grief diet of cigarettes and skinny lattes balanced out by the occasional bag of peanut M&M's, the choked-down fast food eaten in the car. And so we eat with a sad passion, we are piggish and pale blue beneath the severe fluorescent lights of IHOP. We have milk shakes for dessert and we drink them slow and sweet as poison as we ponder the inherent SAT question of IHOP: *Food is to grief as* _____ *is to happiness.*

* * *

And then we are out of the IHOP and into the night and the world glimmers and sways with its many Father Bob Dugans and Catherine Bennetts, and we are stunned all over again by the freezing wind.

Bradley zips up his jacket and walks around the Dumpster for a quick hit and I open my glove box and feel my cold, cold gun.

When Bradley finishes weed patrol and hops in the car, wreathed with smoke, a bitter campfire, I ask, "Do you want to just drive around with me for a while?"

"That's exactly what I want to do, Sandinista," Bradley says. Resplendent in his post-weed calm, he closes his eyes.

We rest for moment, and then I start up the Taurus.

The food is heavy in my stomach and I turn on my wind-shield wipers, trying to break up the little cold stars on my windshield. It's Robert Frost's world, we just live in it. Cruising along the winter streets, I ponder the main events of the week, the details and detritus, the boring baggage of *why why why.*

As I drive, Bradley honors my silence—he doesn't ask any jackassy and/or existential questions like: *Where are we going? Where have we been?* He knows where I will drive, and I'm sure he knows my mind is a wasteland of why and why and why did everyone just act like nothing happened? Why? This is the world Father Bob Dugan and Catherine Bennett invented, and I see them holding hands and waving to the crowd like any politician and his wife who are the leaders of that big country called I Will Never Have to Pay for the Bad Shit That I Do. I Will Keep Smiling Like a Jackass and All Will Smile Back at Me. And behind them is their national flag flipping around in the wind, a free-floating open mouth with squiggles and lightning bolts shooting out, a pair of serpentine lips, puckering up to move in for a juicy Judas kiss.

Bradley looks out his window at nothing, at the chain restaurants and the strip malls, and I know he's thinking of Father Bob—Rahhhbert—and his new boy—the name *Miles* etched on Bradley's brain and hurting his heart; I know he's thinking how the world you know can be yanked out from underneath you and that, my friends, is that.

And there will be nothing left for you, no witness pro-tection program, no kindness or understanding, only bland, blind smiles and people with their teasing *I know/I don't know* vibe, which of course is distilled, crystalline bullshit. Certainly a lot of people knew about the way Catherine Bennett treated Alecia Hardaway, and they never did one thing about it.

Certainly *I* knew; certainly I never did a thing about it.

Maybe it's because I'm still a little Mass-dazzled, but it seems like God is calling me to *act,* to do something.

I cannot turn back the clock. Just as I'm thinking this my brain floods with the image of my mother changing the clocks for daylight saving time and saying, "Jesus, I'm going to be so tired in the morning."

I am not completely powerless.

* * *

And so it seems that my car knows which way to go. The Taurus realizes that it is headed to Catherine Bennett's house. I think how, if we could go back in time, the configuration of the passengers would be different. My mother would be me in the driver's seat, and I would be Bradley in the passenger seat and Bradley would be unknown to me and off on some creepy adventure with Father Bob.

I take the all-too-familiar right-hand turn, and I drive down Ponderosa Lane until I get to Catherine Bennett's house.

Bradley, without asking, knows where we are.

"So this is the teacher's house," he says. He turtles his head across the dark front seat for a better look. The nutcracker is still displayed in her front yard.

"Yes. I thought I'd drop by and see if she wants to go for a cup of hot cocoa with us."

Bradley nods. "I do a lot of drive-bys too."

I think of Bradley driving through the parking lot of Our Lady of Mercedes in his parents' car, of seeing Father Bob's car parked in front of his charming carriage house, a regular car made dazzling by its godly loneliness. But in the parking lot, way in the back next to the Dumpsters behind the church, there is another car, of course. Or perhaps Miles has a moped or maybe a mountain bike. In any case, Bradley is left with the image of the new boy racing through the parking lot, his breath a cold cloud, his unzipped jacket beating against his back. When Bradley looks up at the church, he doesn't experience the comfort of the saints gazing down at him with their exquisite heartaches and unusual martyrdoms; he only sees the impenetrable, well-insured gray windows.

"I don't think she's home," I say, looking at Catherine Bennett's unlit house.

"Okay," he says.

"I'm going to circle around the back, just to check."

And Bradley says, "Oh, okay," with über-cheerfulness, as if my house-stalking is just the thing to do, a perfectly reasonable and legitimate errand, and so despite all my innate despair, I'm feeling pretty happy to have such a nice friend, pretty happy not to be driving down these icy streets alone.

My mind goes hazy and honeyed for a second, but then there is the voice of Catherine Bennett in my ear: *Are you . . . Are you . . . Are you . . .*

And forever is the dead feeling of life being so massively fucked up and everyone going along with all the bullshit. Where is our motherfucking pioneer spirit? What would the saints say, those nutty iconoclasts who gouged out their eyes and jammed swords into their own human hearts?

Navy blue moonlight shines through the trees, and I think of Alecia Hardaway screwing up her face, trying *so* hard to find just the right answer, and a deep, spreading anger blooms in me, a goth-black garden rose with charred and cancerous petals and splashed with pale yellow Pollyanna surprise at the unringing phone. And then there are the thorns of Catherine Bennett's paisley slip, the sight of which was never a victory, only a flag of grotesquerie that forms behind my eyelids like a blood blister, and I take the corner too fast.

There is the dark, stomach-flip thrill of my car fishtailing across the snowy street, the streetlights peering down like brontosaurus heads on their beanpole bodies.

There is the close-up image of my mom dancing around the kitchen in an orange poncho and jeans, and off in the hazy-snow distance there she is again, my mother standing on the street corner, my mother daydreaming and drinking her cappuccino and *Oh, Mom, where* are *you? I love you I love you I do* and then there is the half second of slick wild *ahhhhh*, before Bradley ruins my bliss of black ice by yelling, "Pump the brakes!"

I lean back and brace my arms to the steering wheel—my body seems to know to do this—but I forget to pump the brakes, even with Bradley imploring me to *pump the brakes*.

What I do is slam my foot on the brake, and the car carnival spins, wild and thrilling, before it slides sideways across the street. I lose my grip entirely. My arms give way and my forehead smacks the side window. There is both the chaos of movement and total stillness as pain radiates down my temple. Bradley says, "Jesus!" And it's more a panicked plea than curse, and next comes the slam-danced icy stop before the lurching and crunching.

My glove box pops open, showering the floor with insurance information, cough drops, lipsticks and hair ties, and the box of bullets. My pink gun sails out and lands on the front seat between us. We are at an odd angle; the car has risen up in front like an obese person standing on her heels, struggling for equilibrium.

"Honey," Bradley says. Sometimes my mother called me that, and I think of the honey in a jar my mother bought at the farmers' market, the fat waxy honeycomb planted in the middle. It is my mother's voice I hear when Bradley says it again, her far-off, star-dazzled sweetness.

As he looks over at me from behind his puffy air bag. I feel a thud of pain where my head struck the window and my mouth is warm and salted, filling up fast.

Bradley says, "Hang on."

And here he has *his* miracle moment.

The Taurus is banged up against a tree, two feet off the ground in the front. I am blinded by the air bag in front of me, but when I look out the side window, the unnatural elevation makes me even queasier. But then there is Superman, ungloved hands on the grille, pushing the car off the tree.

With a little rocking, with a snow-filtered *"Fuck!"* from Bradley, the car bounces and aligns. I am back on solid ground.

Bradley opens my door, his cold, labored breath in my face. "Are you okay? I should have gotten you out of the car before I did that. I'm not thinking straight."

Squashed beneath my deflated air bag, I look up at him and smile. I try to say "Superman," but my tongue goes slushy.

"Oh, God," Bradley says. He squints down at me, the wind stirring his bangs. "Can you get out of the car?" And so I do, I stagger out, dizzy and stumbling in my cumbersome platforms. My body is ringing and ringing, the feeling of Catherine Bennett kicking my desk, that vibration amped up and shooting through my limbs, radiating my heart and organs, that part of my body known in the obtuse lingo of yoga classes as my *core,* and it's all *Fuck you fuck you fuck you* and *Wow, so wearing a seat belt is a practice I should probably look into.*

Bradley puts his hands on my shoulders. I blink up at him, at the telephone wires and snowy tree branches, all the refreshing cold after the hot chemical smell of the air bags, the lit-up houses in the distances, sweet as cottages in the Black Forest. It is suddenly very, very important for me to tell him: *The world is brutal but beautiful,* but I can't get the words out.

"Can you spit?" Bradley turns into a bossy dental hygienist and says sternly: "You need to spit, Sandinista." And so I hang open my mouth and lean over. A fat Rorschach of blood stains the snow around my shoes.

Bradley looks down at me, his face so kind and full of worry that I feel a wintry jolt of happiness, and smile.

"Your teeth look a little bloody. Are they okay?"

I run my tongue over my teeth. I wipe my mouth with my hand.

Like a magician, like Cary Grant, Bradley whips a handkerchief from his back pocket and blots my face with it. I think of church—the cloth swiped over the goblet.

"My teeth are fine!" I say triumphantly. I lean over and spit into the snow again. "I think I just bit my tongue or my lip or something." I run my tongue over my teeth again. "My teeth are exactly the same!"

"Okay," Bradley says. "We better get out of here."

He takes me gently by the shoulder and helps me back into the car, where the air bags are already deflating, drooping like ancient breasts. He walks around to the driver's side, pausing to look at the grill and saying, "Shit," under his breath.

He pulls open the door and gives me the news: "The front of your car is pretty messed up. But I think it's still drivable." He shuts his car door. "Jesus."

"Yeah," I say, as if blaming the so-called savior or pleading with him like some imperiled Bible-beater. "Jesus Christ."

Bradley runs his hand over his neck and says, "I don't know if we should call your insurance company, or do we need to file an accident report with the police—"

"Let's just go," I say. "Let's just move."

Bradley nods and pulls the spent air bag to the middle of

the front seat. It has sprouted from the center of the steering wheel that hangs open like a stunned mouth; there's no honking my horn now.

The gun falls from the front seat to the floor.

"Whoops-a-daisy!" I say, my voice saccharine and strained.

Bradley reaches to the floorboards with a wince, giving up a little *ugh* of pain as he grabs the gun. It gleams in his hand, pink and white as Easter. He chuckles under his breath, before he says, slowly and instructionally, "Of course, we should probably get rid of the *gun* if we are considering calling the police to report the accident."

"Probably," I agree.

"Where did you get it?" he asks, frowning at the candied handle.

"It's a bit of a long story, but I got it at Second Chance?"

"Arne sold you a gun?" Bradley snorts. "Jesus, that guy's a stone-cold freak."

"No. I mean, he didn't sell it to me. He gave it to me. It was a gift. A donation. And he's not a freak, either."

"Guess what?" Bradley says quietly. "That's even weirder: that he *gave* you a gun. Do you have a license for it?"

"Well, you know, not as yet. To tell you the truth, Bradley, I didn't know that you needed a license for a gun." I try to downplay the weirdness of this postcrash talk with humor. "Now that I think about it, that policy strikes me as highly un-American."

"Well, aren't you quite the patriot." He reaches down and takes the box of bullets off the car floor. "These flew out and hit my knee like a boulder."

"Sorry," I mutter.

He looks at the box. "You know, these are not bullets for a handgun. This is deer-hunting ammo. These bullets wouldn't fit in your gun." He chuckles. "God bless Arne. He probably wanted you to have the gun so you would feel safe, but not actually be able to harm anyone. Yourself included. You never tried to put the bullets in?"

"Well, no," I say, a little testy, ever the duped and dumb girl. "For safety reasons I didn't want to load it before I needed to use it."

Bradley frowns.

So. How could I have known those bullets wouldn't work in my gun? The culture of violence is new to me; my mother would not kill a bug. If she found a daddy longlegs in the house, she would pick it up and cup it in her bare hands; she would giggle and scold it. "You stop! That tickles!" I would stand at the kitchen window and watch my mother crouch down in the backyard, the sun in her hair, and open her hands for the spider. *Wow,* I would think, *what a freaking nutjob.*

Bradley switches on the dome light, examines the gun with his eyes squinted in concentration, like a jeweler. "The serial number has been sanded off. This is nobody's gun. But it's highly illegal."

He puts the gun on the seat and drums his fingers along the top of the steering wheel before he starts up the car, and I'm thinking that the stress of this night will make him hit the ganja pretty hard. He smokes way too much; I see that it affects his decision making, though probably I shouldn't judge.

"You know, in any case, a gun isn't the smartest item to be toting around in your car."

This from someone never without a bag of weed!

"I *know.* But thanks for the tip."

He looks into the rearview mirror, and then opens the car door. He flings my gun into the banked snow; he heaves the box of bullets out with a wince.

"Hey! What—"

"Sorry. Just an impulse."

"But Jesus, it's mine. The gun was a *gift,*" I say, as if I'm wearing a pink frilly dress and have fluffy curls. I notice that my whole trunk hurts, not just my rib.

"The last thing you need is a gun," Bradley says.

As if we are so different, as if he's suddenly a bearded sage sitting cross-legged on a hilltop, meditating and eating unsweetened yogurt whereas I'm a random meth head swilling Dr Pepper for my sugar jones, having sex with strangers for quick cash.

"Well, Bradley, what's the first thing I need?" My face is sleeved in pain. I touch my hand to my forehead and feel the Cro-Magnon bump. "Could you perchance tell me the *seventeenth* thing I need?"

Bradley ignores me. As we drive off, the Taurus pulls to the left, so Bradley has to constantly correct it with sharp little turns to the right, but it drives. It will get us home.

* * *

So it's good-bye to my gun-girl self. But say I really *wanted* to get a gun. Say I sought out bullets that worked, that were the right fit. How hard would that be? Given that I didn't even know I wanted a gun in the first place? Given that I learned I have the gift of good aim?

* * *

Bradley takes the interstate downtown, the car miraculously chug-chug-chugging away in the slow lane, the little mid-sized economy car that could. He drives us to Thirty-Eighth Street, where the Pale Circus glows with its warm lit windows, with the headless mannequin and her implicit scare-crow's lament: *If I only had a brain.*

"Back to work?" I say.

Bradley tries for a bit of levity. He sings the *Snow White* song: "Heigh-ho, heigh-ho, it's back to work we go!"

But with the spent air bag brushing my sore legs, with no gun amping up my badass self, I think of Snow White in her agony, Walt Disney's poisoned princess laid out in her clear coffin, wearing her yellow dress with the starched collar, awaiting a kiss. And of course Catherine Bennett appears in my mind, holding up her teacher's textbook like a poisoned apple, smiling at Alecia Hardaway, at me.

Bradley parks, gets out of the car and walks over to my side, gallant and limping. He motions for me to unroll the window.

"I'm going to try out my neighborhood connections," he says with a wink.

I roll up my window and watch him lope across the snowy street, my sore head pressed to the glass. He goes into the liquor store; through the front windows it looks like a blurred carnival of boozy light and moving bodies, as if in the midst of a late-night clearance sale. There is just enough light to see a monk coming out of Erika's Erotic Confections. He has his head lowered, his hood up. He waits on the sidewalk next to Erika's car. And out comes Erika: jeans tucked into storm-trooper snow boots and a leather jacket with the collar flipped up. She has her purse on her shoulder, but it slips to the crook of her arm when she turns and locks the metal door of her shop.

The monk stares down at the sidewalk, which the soft new snow has turned to silk. I cup my hand to my sore mouth and touch my puffed lips, watching. Erika and the monk exchange no words. With his hands in his robe pockets, the monk watches her get in her car and drive away. Perhaps what they are giving each other is more than forbidden, starlit romance; perhaps it's not that at all, but the protection of friendship. The monk stands on the sidewalk until Erika's car lights fade into the darkness. And then he trudges up snowy Thirty-Eighth Street in his sandals, heading for home.

Bradley comes out of the liquor store triumphant, flashing a thumbs-up sign as he slip-slides across the street, brown bag raised over his head like a bowling trophy. Not cool: if any undercover cops are lurking, we are further screwed. I haul my sorry self out of the car, and together we cross the frozen sidewalk in front of the Pale Circus.

I take a quick look back at my car, the crunched front end. From behind you would never know anything was wrong. And I mourn my mother yet again as I remember using fingernail polish remover and a putty knife to take off her embarrassing, self-aggrandizing bumper stickers: KEEP YOUR THEOLOGY OFF MY BIOLOGY, THANK GODDESS, THE ONLY BUSH I TRUST IS MY OWN. I wish I'd left them on, in memoriam, instead of scraping them off, because the bumper stickers were a sign of my mother's essence. The bottle of lemon-scented fingernail polish remover and the putty knife, well, that was pure me: Little Miss Lemming.

Bradley takes a ring of keys from his jacket pocket and unlocks the front door.

"Let there be light," he says, his voice grandiose as Vegas Elvis's.

And he flips the switch and here is the glorious landscape of cotton and wool and acetate, satin against the night sky, and yes it's lovely, but I'm thinking *My gun my gun oh my sweet gun.* And Catherine Bennett smiles and says, *Have you been paying attention?*

Does no one understand how completely easy it is to get a gun? Will no one give me an ounce of respect?

Bradley puts the brown bag on the cash desk. He takes off his jacket and rubs his elbows as he looks at the thermostat. He turns up the heat, which will take a long time to kick in. Bradley takes the bottle—champagne—and two plastic cups out of the bag. He pops the cork, and champagne bubbles up and spills on the gleaming hardwood floors. Both of us go lurching for the paper towels beneath the register; Henry Charbonneau has us trained.

Bradley snaps a square of paper towel off the roll and wipes up the spilled champagne. Then he folds two paper towels into elegant octagons and hands me one. I pour the champagne and we raise our cups in a mock-glamorous toast, our aching arms linked. He looks at me very seriously, as if he might cry, and says, "Sandinista, we survived the car wreck—"

And here he seems like a drama mama most supreme, because a car careening off a suburban street and smacking into a cottonwood tree is rarely a death sentence. It is just what it is, some bad luck, just like the Cutlass that jumped the curb and killed my mother was pure bad luck and Catherine Bennett was—is—Alecia Hardaway's bad luck. Or do we have the power to change fate? If not our own, someone else's?

I blot my hurt lips with the paper towel and come away with a red-russet stain, the color of an autumn lipstick.

Bradley puts his hand on my shoulder and says, "We survived the car wreck. And had I died, oh, it would be tragic, heaven knows, and Robert could do my funeral Mass, he could plant the old Judas kiss on my embalmed lips and whisk me off to heaven."

"He would certainly weep for your handsome young corpse."

"I hope he would slit his throat," Bradley says dreamily, staring off at a canary-yellow coat on a display form, the genius of its jeweled white buttons, the softly flared collar. "But really, it's only important that you didn't die, Sandinista. You are . . . the last of your tribe. Which I realize is a corn-dog thing to say—add a root beer float and order of fries and you're good to go, Miss. But, you are . . . the last."

I feel my throat close, so I take a long drink of champagne.

"And so the whole business with the gun—which is your business, granted—it just seems like a bad idea. You can't do anything that is going to *hurt you.*"

And there's a lot of *h* in his *hurt.* It is a long, awkward softness of *hhhhh.* The sound of it makes my mouth hurt even more.

I'm afraid he's going to cry; I'm afraid I'm going to cry, so I take the wheel and drive us off this steep road. I say: "You know, I thought you were in love with Henry Charbonneau. I thought I picked up that vibe."

"No," Bradley says sadly. "God, no. Did you really think I would find his dissertations about the proper way to Swiffer for maximum detritus pickup to be some sort of red-hot aphrodisiac? Give me some credit, Sandinista."

"True, his cleaning advice is a bit of a cold shower. But technically he's so beautifully handsome," I say.

"Technically, yes, he is," Bradley says. "Last summer when I first started working here, we almost kissed one time when we were both drunk. We were, like, a half centimeter away from it. But then Henry Charbonneau said, 'Do you want me to burn in hell for all of eternity? Go forth and live your life with fellow young people.' Do you know that he's positive?"

I look at my fancy, snow-stained shoes and take another gulp of champagne. "That *sucks.* But, can't you live, like, for fifty years on all the good medicines they have now? The new HIV cocktails?"

Bradley shrugs. "Well, *sure,*" he says, his voice charged with sarcasm. "But still, it would trouble a person. It's still kind of a bullshit thing to have at the back of your mind all day long: *I have HIV. Will my medicine let me live for fifty years?*"

And I'm thinking who in their right mind would want to live for another fifty years, and also: *What is wrong with me?* "Right," I say. "It's terrible. Of course it's a terrible weight." I take another sip.

"Although Henry Charbonneau is filthy rich, so there's that," Bradley says. "He can get the best medical care. He's Mr. Trust Fund."

He runs his tongue over his chapped lips, a brief comfort. With his finger and crucified thumb, he pulls away a flake of dead skin. "Still, anyway, when I take money from the register I always pay it back. Even though Henry Charbonneau doesn't need the money from the Pale Circus to live on; it probably doesn't even pay for his personal dry cleaning. I pay it all back anyway."

And I know this isn't quite true, but it doesn't matter to me in the least. "Borrowing isn't stealing," I say, and Bradley could not agree more.

* * *

By the time we finish off the bottle, we both feel a lot less sore. The champagne gives us a kick of *wheeeee!* And all the sublime colors of the Pale Circus pinwheel through my mind, the blues and lavenders, the soft cherry-pinks and groovy greens. We sit in front of the display window and stare out at our white city, the velvety snow-globe fantasy of it all.

Bradley looks down at my platforms and says, "Take off your shoes."

And I take them off, thinking of all the little adventures my shoes have known today, envisioning them on the shelf of a secondhand store, how the next person who owns them will not know that they hold the energy of candy-pink guns, of Catherine Bennett and car crashes.

Bradley stumbles over to the shoe display and brings back a pair of ski boots from the shelf; they are wide and fat as marshmallows and my feet squish around in them. I have to admit they feel better than my platforms. He's changed out of his shoes too; he's wearing the Ziggy Stardust boots with his jeans tucked in.

He puts his hand down and helps me up. "And now we go," he says dramatically. I do not ask where we're going; I let Bradley lead me to the door. Bradley locks up the store with great effort, as if masterfully solving a Rubik's Cube. I look across the street and see three guys in army fatigues and berets getting out of a car in front of the liquor store. They're joking around—one guy using hand gestures to tell a story as his friends laugh. They don't look much older than me, so maybe they are nineteen-year-olds on leave from Iraq in search of alcoholic beverages. No matter, if they aren't twenty-one yet they'll have to rely on their uniforms or a decent fake ID to buy their beer.

"Ready?" Bradley puts out his hand and we take a few steps together. Even in my flat boots, I have to extend one hand for balance, as if I am surfing.

We are far too drunk to drive.

It seems like we should call a taxi, make a plan, but we both take off purposefully down the icy sidewalk, though we've nowhere to go. The cold air and the champagne have transformed my sadness to pure, crystalline melancholia, as if I could step in front of a city bus and feel no pain, only the inevitability of the day's second accident. And yet, the army guys offer up a little jolt of reality: Why have I assumed I can't go to Europe without my mother? Given that I could be off on some dangerous mission to Afghanistan or Iraq, would it really be such a burden to visit fashion capitals and coastal towns by myself?

It would be a little sad. That's all.

Bradley stumbles a bit on an icy patch, and when I put my arm out for him, we hold hands for a moment. He looks across the street at the liquor store and says, "Wait here."

I'm thinking that going off for more booze is not the hottest idea that Bradley has ever had, when he grabs two cardboard boxes from a heap in front of the liquor store. He quickly breaks them down into flat, slatted squares, my sweet recycler extraordinaire. He doesn't bother to look before he crosses the street, his head tucked against the cold winds.

When he hands me a square of cardboard I smile. "Thanks?" And then he takes my hand.

"Let's roll, Sandinista," Bradley says. And so we walk up Thirty-Eighth Street together, past the deserted brick building with chained, gated windows that look doleful and resigned, yet full of dignity: these buildings that have simply said *Fuck it* and closed in on themselves. No wallflower hopes of urban renewal for these aged beauties, no weather-beaten, delusional real estate signs, AVAILABLE FOR LEASE OR SALE, PLEASE CALL . . .

Please call. Pleasecallpleasecall.

Yes, I suppose I am *paying attention.*

Thirty-Eighth Street shines icy and virginal against the streetlights. We are huffing and puffing, chugging up the sidewalk like the drunken smokers that we are, and my body starts to ache again: my lips, my forehead, my back, neck, and also that spot on my ribs, a pulsing pain on my ribs, though that bruise is fading. But when we reach the top of the street, when we're standing in front of St. Joseph's Monastery, looking down, it is the smallest victory, our breath fat and plumed. Bradley says, "Let's go." And I follow him through the side yard of the monastery, cardboard slapping at the packed snow.

Bright floodlights switch on, trapping us in a rhombus of golden light. Bradley looks handsome and electric and we freeze like startled, experimental lovers: *Uh, what exactly are we doing?*

I ask Bradley, "Will we be arrested for trespassing?"

"They'll definitely forgive us," Bradley says. We go scrambling out of the side yard, into the safe, snowy darkness at the back of the monastery. There is a steep hill that slopes dramatically with swirled untracked snow. Lit by the moon, it looks like white sand, and I see now what Bradley is after.

"Well, so . . ." I assess the packed snow that rises into the brick wall of the monastery. I hold up my cardboard. "If we freak out and sled right into the brick wall . . . that would be kind of bad news, yes?"

In profile Bradley lit by the winter moon is so beautiful—his breath a cold cloud that forms and re-forms—and the champagne still so awhirl in my brain that I lose my own monastic aesthetic and wish things could be different; I wish I could put my cold, hurt mouth on his. He looks over at me for a long, bizarre second, and maybe I'm drunkenly imagining it, but Bradley seems to be thinking the same thing. But then he flashes me a big, warm smile and ambles up the hill like a freaking billy goat. He sticks the cardboard under one arm, and wings his other arm out, elbow bent, and calls out, "Bawwk bawwk bawwk."

"Monsieur Maturity," I say. "And FYI? I am not a chicken."

"Sandinista, you *so* don't have to tell me that."

And so the odd moment is buried and I trek up the hill, stiff-kneed as Frankenstein's monster. The snow and the ink sky look like an indigo vintage dress so beautiful that I would wear it on my wedding day—and I'm entertaining many drunken thoughts about the juxtaposition of purity and darkness when Bradley calls down the hill to me, whisper-yelling so as not to wake the sleeping monks: "Get moving, girl. God! You're such a slowpoke!"

Inevitably I lose my balance and fall on the new snow that only looks like swirls of soft-serve ice cream; there is black ice beneath.

"Fuck!" I say. And then of course I feel bad when I look at the snow-crowned stone saint in the corner, as if he is about to come to life—Frosty the Snowman with a Christ obsession—and run shrieking into the streets at my profanity.

And of course when I fell, my piece of cardboard, my "sled," went sailing down the hill with a gritty whoosh, off into the night. There's no way I'm going after it.

"You okay?" Bradley calls down the hill.

"Oh, I'm great," I mumble. "Fanfuckingtastic."

When I finally make it to the top of the incline, Bradley holds out his hand to me. "Here, my dear."

"You have a lot of good ideas," I tell him, taking his hand. "Such as monastery sledding in the dark."

"Oh, like *you* don't have any crazy ideas?"

We're silent for a moment, admiring the night.

"It's funny," I finally say, "how there's all this snow, some kind of Antarctica supreme, and yet it's not really that cold—it's brisk, more like spring."

"These are the halcyon days of global warming," Bradley agrees. "It's not like when we were little, standing at the bus stop with your lungs raspy from breathing in the freezing air, and your face feels frozen, like you can't take it for another second, and then the bus finally comes rolling down the street."

And I think it's not only global warming but that other thing too: that you lose your milk teeth and your perfect baby skin, that you lose your mother and you learn that you just have to take it, you have to feel it. There is nothing else.

Except for Bradley, who drops his cardboard on the snow and braces it with his Ziggy Stardust boot, a snow-kissed storm trooper, the hero of my own little winter wonderland.

"Looks like somebody's riding bitch," he says, employing

a tough straight-guy accent, macho with earthy, redneck undertones.

Together we sit down on the cardboard, a scramble of legs and arms. Close to him now, I feel only the warmth of friendship, of family. And so we sit at the top of the monks' backyard for a second, at ease, our boots parallel to the cardboard, anchoring us to the snow.

We enjoy our aerial view of the city—*Look! Look how pretty! The lit-up sign for the VFW hall, those retro flashing consonants. Look at the top floor of the new circular condominiums lit up like a concrete layer cake, and look up there, at the single light that has switched on in the third floor of the monastery.* I wonder: Is it a monk with a stomachache? Perhaps an insomniac flipping through his Bible or playing solitaire? Maybe just a random fellow pilgrim waking with the bad feeling of *uh-oh uh-oh uh-oh uh-oh.*

"Look," Bradley says, but I'm already looking: a bearded monk has appeared at the window. Did he hear us? Could he sense us in the snowy darkness? He's not sporting his monk apparel, he's wearing a white T-shirt and could pass as anybody's grandpa about to raise the window to call out, "I see you crazy kids out there! You're going to break your goddamn necks sledding in the darkness."

But he doesn't. He raises his hands and places them, palms out on the window. He bows his head. And then he is gone, the light switched off.

Remember, the King of Kings will be there with you.

I put my hand into my pocket and pick out my wrinkly little Eucharist wafer. I bow my head and sneak it into my mouth. Without speaking, we—*we!* the sweetest of pronouns—pull our feet off the snow at the same time and the sled takes off with a *swoooosh,* my arms around Bradley, Christ in my mouth and birds in my stomach as we fly into morning.

sunday

THIS IS THE DAY THE LORD HAS MADE

I open my eyes and realize it's a day with two mornings: the snow-shadowed dawn and right now, in my bed, with Bradley next to me. The champagne bubbles have turned to lead and bob freely in my temples; the dusty digital clock on my nightstand tells me that it's 10:56. In approximately four minutes the alarm will go off and with a full three hours of beauty sleep, Bradley and I will rise and shower and eat a little something before we work the Sunday shift at the Pale Circus: noon to five, people, and in honor of the Day of the Lord, your second item is half off. We took a cab home last night, given our champagne consumption, and so we'll have to take one to the Pale Circus this morning. I know my car is still drivable, but wonder how I will get the crunched grille fixed. My mother had a mechanic—his name was Russell—but where does he work? Adding another detail to the slate of my life makes me want to sleep for a hundred days.

Instead I roll over and study Bradley's arm slung across the pillow, the hairs and freckles, the dry skin, the veins in his hands, the crucifix on his thumb, a dark bruise on his elbow. I watch the shallow rise and fall of his chest, the fading moment of his nocturnal delicacy. I touch my tongue to my swollen lip and think how I can perhaps coat it, gently, with dark lipstick and pass it off as a bad collagen injection. My second thought is how strange it is to have a body, to not just be a collection of random floating thoughts, but to own a solid little patch of the universe. My own body has changed; it has absorbed the pain of the past months. For those first weeks after my mother died, I would wake up happy enough in the bright spell of the first split second of day. But that flash of ignorance was never bliss, given the reality that would follow, the electric blue shock of it all.

And now my body has absorbed this other surprise. I know the school will not call.

I miss my gun.

But Bradley is awake now, and humming, a small smile on his face, his eyes still closed. The sun slashes through the inch between the window frame and the shade, shooting in a line of snow-white brightness. Bradley reaches across the bed and takes my hand, and we lie there like chaste, realistic honeymooners who will never divorce. He sings out slowly, softly: "This is the day the Lord has made, let us rejoice and be glad in it."

Bradley sings with his eyes closed, maybe not such a bad idea, since the stripe of sun highlights the dust in my room. It is no mere speckling on my walnut dresser and bureau, it is thick and white, the stray fluff of a cottonwood tree on the clock radio and jewelry box and picture frames. I have not swiped a cloth over anything since my mother died. And so she is with us here in the bedroom, her dry skin and dandruff, her skin cells and hair. Of course the throwaway detritus of a human being is the lamest of consolations. Still, it's better than nothing. I tilt my head back on the pillow and look at the framed cross-stitch over my bed. My mother made it when she was into embroidery—a blissfully quick phase, as seeing her on the sofa with her little wooden hoop and Baggie of colorful threads—*Hello, Ma Ingalls!*—always vexed me. She loved trying out new art projects—knitting, painting, beading, ceramics, printmaking, and my least favorite, weaving, which involved a large rickety loom that briefly took up residence in our living room like a cumbersome hippie roommate. Our DIY home decor is an homage to her craftiness, but the cross-stitch sampler hanging over my bed is all that remains of her winter of embroidery. It's definitely corny, but I won't take it down. Because, once upon a time, my mother sat on the couch, and with needle and soft blue thread, embroidered the only prayer she believed in:

PRAYER FOR THE CARE OF CHILDREN
Almighty God, Heavenly Father,
You have blessed us

With the joy and care of children:
Give us calm strength and patient wisdom
As we bring them up,
So that we may teach them to love
Whatever is just and true and good,
Following the example of our Savior,
Jesus Christ.

—The Book of Common Prayer, 1979

Bradley is still singing in a high, goosey voice: "This is the day the Lord has made, let us rejoice and be glad in it."

Clearly this is an anthem for the deluded or the mentally ill; I suppose we are both.

"This is the day the Lord has made, let us rejoice and be glad in it, let us rejoice, let us rejoice, let us rejoice and be glad in it."

Possibly this is the lamest song ever, made bearable only by Bradley's ironic crooning.

But then Bradley opens his eyes and sings in his regular voice: "This is the day the Lord has made, let us rejoice and be glad in it." His voice is clean, strong. I imagine the bad priest picking his voice out of the choir, letting his eyes flutter shut while he listened to Bradley sing. Jesus, if he is at the helm, if he really exists beyond the spun-sugar Milky Way of stained glass and mahogany pews, would not look down in fey, helpless confusion; he would admit he is doing a highly questionable job of shepherding his flock. He would, in the words of daytime TV, *own it.*

But when I think of Jesus hanging on the cross at

Bradley's church, his face is not just the standard ostentatious suffering, Jesus rendered as the big wooden crybaby of Our Lady of Mercedes. The Son of God looks confused and highly pissed: *Big Daddy's grandiose plans have gotten me into a bit of a pickle.*

And I think of my mother, her rejection of all things Catholic and our subsequent church-hopping, her tiresome rants about the patriarchal hijacking of Christianity. And yet, she always told me: "Jesus is your brother." It's what she believed: *Jesus is my brother.* Nobody could take that away from her.

As we lie there together, I start to sing along with Bradley: "This is the day the Lord has made, let us rejoice and be glad in it, let us rejoice, let us rejoice, let us rejoice and be glad in it"—the chorus of the next thirty seconds until the alarm goes off—"be glad in it be glad in it be glad in it."

* * *

After a rush of customers, the store is suddenly quiet. Late afternoon: Bradley's in the back alley, on his Pale Circus smoke break. Unable to control myself, I decide to call home and check my messages one more time. Because what the hell, and also because I'm not really expecting a call on a Sunday. People are at church or reading the newspaper or arguing with their family about the day's chores; nobody can hurt me on a Sunday. According to the Lord it's the first day of the week, but it always feels like the last. In kindergarten I had underpants embroidered with the days of the week, and I liked it when Sunday came, the navy blue cursive letters, and the comfort of the week finishing, the closure of a spaghetti dinner and a bubble bath, fingernails trimmed and hair shampooed before Monday morning, when the world reliably began anew.

I'm standing at the counter, the cell phone jammed between my ear and my shoulder, when I hear the five words that start my heart shuddering: "You have one new message."

I punch in 617. My mother's birthday was June seventeenth. How could I ever forget my code? I'm looking at a round rack of candy-colored sweaters when I hear: "Sandinista, this is Lisa Kaplansky."

I close my eyes and the colorful sweaters form a brief, bright rainbow on my eyelids.

"Hey, I was out of school last week from Tuesday through Friday—my baby got sick on Monday night—it started out as just a regular flu, with a fever, but evolved into full-blown pneumonia. Charlie ended up in the hospital for two nights—nightmare—but he's fine now, so I'll be back at school in the morning. And I heard that there was a problem with Catherine Bennett last Monday? Listen, come to my room first thing in the morning and we'll try to get it sorted out. Okay? I'll be looking for you. Okay, Sandinista. Hope you're well. Bye."

It happened.

Finally.

I am shaking. I take a deep breath and run my tongue over my lip, coming away with a taste of dried blood and lipstick, while my mind zooms: Lisa Kaplansky. Lisa Kaplansky. And Monday. And school? Going back to school? Because I'm on the schedule at the Pale Circus from ten to five on Monday. What would I tell Henry Charbonneau?

Especially after this morning, when I found a gorgeous comfort waiting for me at the Pale Circus: a note from Henry pinned to the mulberry ball gown that was displayed in the front window at the beginning of the week.

> *Sandinista, I thought this would be just the thing for you. Wear it with glee. Love, Henry C.*

When I tried the dress on, I was surprised at how perfect it looked on me, as if I had clicked my heels three times and turned into a 1950s starlet. For Bradley, Henry left a dove-gray shirt with a collar that flared out in deep, handsome Vs and fit as if custom-tailored in Milan.

Bradley and I, though achy from the car accident, vamped together in the three-way mirror: "You're gorgeous." "No, you are!" And then, just as our heads started to throb from the world in general and specifically from a lack of caffeine, Erika showed up with two lattes in a cardboard carrier. Of course she brought chocolates for the candy dish, because that's Erika's thing, her job, but the coffee was a specific kindness that required seven dollars and twenty minutes out of her morning to stop at Buzz Café, to jostle hot beverages across a snowy street. She did a double take when she saw my swollen lip, because makeup only does so much: "Sandinista?" Her voice gentle but laced with panic.

"Driving on the ice?" Bradley said quickly, and he put his hand on Erika's back. "Not really Sandinista's strong suit."

"Oh," she said. She laughed a little. "Okay. That's right. I saw your car out there."

In this fifteen-second exchange, I saw that Bradley knew the backstory of Erika's assault. I saw how quickly he moved to reassure her—and with just the right tone—that the same thing hadn't happened to me. And then time stopped and roared past all at once as I projected him into his confident, happy adult life in a different city—Manhattan or Málaga—a man holding a book, a baguette, a man with a suit and a smile, without the weed, without the bad priest. I wanted to tell him that his cleverness and imagination would take him far and that none of his kindness had been wasted, but that's a tricky thing to say. When Erika left the store, what I actually said was: "Bradley? Seriously? That shirt really does look terrific on you."

And now: it has happened. I've gotten the call, and my heart is full of Lisa Kaplansky's words; oh, how easily they translate into those highlighted words from my mother's junior high Bible: *I will not leave you comfortless; I will come to you.* And I think of Erika, hard-core and sweet and broken, and of Henry Charbonneau, seemingly all froth and delicious eyes and ludicrous asides. Yet Henry Charbonneau has his own bullshit deal dogging his days: HIV. And still they both give thoughtful gifts; they both pay attention. I look over my shoulder and admire my calves in the thin mirror on the end of the shoe rack—I've borrowed black beaded satin pumps from the shoe rack, and the three-inch heels do something crazy fantastic to my legs. It seems that vanity is an antidote to any residual grief, until I think of my mother, lacing up her espadrilles as she sat on the edge of her bed before taking a long, cool look at herself in the mirror, smiling at her own yogalicious calves.

I walk to the back of the Pale Circus and take yet another good look at myself in the three-way mirror: the lavender-gray shadows under my eyes, my banged-up mouth. Beneath my fanciful dress, the bruise on my ribs—Monday's surprise—has faded to a shadow. It has been a long week, and there's still work to be done. Along with my dress and Bradley's shirt, Henry Charbonneau left a very long list of Sunday chores written out in pastel-colored pencil: marshmallow-pink, mint-green and baby chick–yellow, as if this would make scrubbing the toilet and changing out the roach motels Easter-sweet. I bitched a bit about the work; I inquired about what Henry Charbonneau might be doing with his free Sunday: refinishing the white pine floors of his loft? Scrambling eggs and chopping fresh chive? Balling melon? Brewing jasmine tea? Bradley smiled and shook his head. He put his hands together, crucified thumb to his heart, and said: "On the seventh day, he rested."

And now Bradley is walking back into the Pale Circus. His eyes are a bit bloodshot and he's forgotten to stamp his feet at the door, tracking in a dusting of snow that would make Henry Charbonneau weep. Bradley rubs his hands together and makes a blustery *brrrr* sound before he looks at me and says, "Sandinista? What? Why are you smiling?"

I can hardly get the words out. "My English teacher called me."

"She did?" Bradley packs the two words with all the tenderness the world has ever known. "She did?"

* * *

I'm Windexing the windows, the Pale Circus filling with that clean, aqua-blue smell, when I see a monk walking down the street. He walks with great purpose, cradling something in his brown robe like a baby. When I lean closer to the window, my forehead resting on the cold pane, I see that it is Brother Bill of the Dixie Cup humor. He stops to look at the crunched-up front end of my Taurus, which is parked right outside the Pale Circus. He brushes off the snow, fools with one of my windshield wipers, and puts something on the hood of my car.

Just as I'm about to open the door and yell out: "Brother Bill, can I help you?" or "Dude, what the hell are you doing to my car?" or some amalgamation of the two, he looks up, twists his head around, then racewalks back down the street to the monastery, his hands tucked up in the folds of his robes.

"I'm stepping outside for a minute," I call out to Bradley, who is dusting, or about to start: he rolls the wooden end of the feather duster between his palms so that the feathers do a slow fan dance. Bradley stares down at the duster with a shy smile, as if he's holding his bridal bouquet. His cell phone is sandwiched between his head and bent neck.

"What?" Bradley startles and drops the feather duster.

"Sorry! I'm going outside."

" 'Kay," Bradley says amicably, offering up a little wave. He smiles, then curls his head down like a cat and whispers something into his phone. Whoever he is talking to makes him laugh, soft and slow. I won't ask.

I pull open the door of the Pale Circus and walk across the snowy sidewalk to my car, cold in my bare dress and holding out one hand for balance. I visor my other hand over my eyes and take a long look at Brother Bill scurrying down Thirty-Eighth Street. And then, when I look down at the hood of my crushed car, I see the monk's gift.

It nearly blinds me.

The sun flares off the brass lid of a mason jar of red jam. I pick it up and look at the jam sparkling beyond the glass, the seeded clots of berry like a chambered heart. There is no label on the jar, no price or bar code, no list of ingredients. There is only a preprinted note card attached to the jar that says LOVE AND BLESSINGS TO YOU FROM YOUR FRIENDS AT ST. JOSEPH'S MONASTERY. The label smells hotly of glue. I brush the lid against my mouth, the ridged metal gold and sweet as a kiss.

I close my eyes for a second, savoring this day of gifts, and for once I do not see Catherine Bennett. I only see Alecia Hardaway under the fluorescent lights in the school corridor, the brilliance of her puzzled smile as she closes her locker and turns to look at me. She's waving, pleasantly at first: *Hi, Sandinista! You're a real cool person, Sandinista! You're a real cool person every day!* But then she starts to wave as if she's drowning: *Look at me, Sandinista! Help me, Sandinista!*

And so I imagine myself showing up on the Hardaways' doorstep. Her mother answers the door and it's me, the real me, resplendent in a white angora sweater and pencil skirt, a lipsticked pinup saint spilling God's truth. *Your daughter is being tormented at school. And not by some random bitchy girl, Mrs. Hardaway. Not by a student. By a teacher. Everyone acts like it doesn't happen. But I have seen it. I've seen it many times, Mrs. Hardaway.* The pinks and purples and wild navy blues of Mrs. Bennett's slip exit my brain, my eyelids. Birds of peace appear on the telephone wires above our heads.

But the valiant holiness of my confession is lost on Mrs. Hardaway. *Tell me how long this has been going on. Tell me!*

All year, I tell her, my voice loud as dinner theater. *Since school started.*

At first her face falls. Mrs. Hardaway chews her lip, maybe thinking of the days when Alecia was at school and she was at work, or sipping a latte or playing computer solitaire or listlessly wandering the aisles of Target, whatever mothers do in those long, lost hours without their children.

But then Mrs. Hardaway says: *And you're just telling me now! You let her suffer just like everyone else for all this time?*

I try to be plucky. *Better late than never! I've been trying to figure out what to do about the teacher. I had a pink gun, but now it's gone. If I get another one, I will take care of Catherine Bennett for you.*

Mrs. Hardaway screams it loud enough for the whole neighborhood to hear: *JESUS CHRIST!*

And of course it's Jesus I'm thinking about as I stand on Thirty-Eighth Street, how all of Christianity seems a cautionary tale, a bleak epiphany visited upon the King of Kings himself as he was nailed to the cross: *What the hell? I guess you can't save anyone else without crucifying yourself.*

But what can any of us do but try? In the morning, I will go to school and talk with Lisa Kaplansky. I will tell her about Alecia. About me.

I stand here on the street for another moment, shivering in my ball gown as I watch Brother Bill trudge up the steep, frozen steps of St. Joseph's. I press the jar of jam to the deep V in the front of my dress, to my bare and bony sternum. It's still warm.

I don't think he sees me.

I *know* he doesn't see me. But then, just before Brother Bill disappears into the monastery, he turns around. He raises his hand, and he waves.

ACKNOWLEDGMENTS

A world of gratitude to Sara Eckel, Lisa Bankoff, Michelle Poploff, Rebecca Short, Angela Carlino, Mary Wharff, Lucia Orth, Laura Moriarty, Judy Bauer, Andrea Hoag, Sharon Zehr, Kellie Wells, Jerald Walker, Whitney Terrell, Jennifer Lawler, Laura Kirk and Stefanie Olson.

And thank you to my family, my parents, my siblings, my husband and my children: I love you all.

MARY O'CONNELL is a graduate of the Iowa Writers' Workshop and the author of the short-story collection *Living with Saints.* Her short fiction and essays have appeared in several literary magazines, and she is the recipient of a James Michener Fellowship and a *Chicago Tribune* Nelson Algren Award. *The Sharp Time* is her first novel.